MARIAN EXALL

A SLIPPERY SLOPE

A Sarah McKinney Mystery

Acknowledgments:

I am more grateful than they could possibly know to Nancy
Bartlett, Dawn Landau, Lynn McKinster and Oona Sherman.
Their advice, criticism and encouragement during the writing
of this novel were invaluable. Thanks also to my family,
especially Graham, without whose support this venture
would not be possible.

A SLIPPERY SLOPE

A Sarah McKinney Mystery

Chapter 1

I was the only customer in the restaurant, so I couldn't help but notice as the maitre d' seated him – inexplicably, given the many options - at the table directly across from mine. He was in his forties, I'd say. Stocky build, grey hair shaved to a quarter inch all over to mask a receding hairline, a healthy, ruddy face, pleasant-looking. He wore a dark blue open-neck shirt under a leather jacket, and well-cut black pants. The jacket was supple lambskin in an unusual light grey shade. I pegged him for a northern European, Belgian or German perhaps. He looked well-groomed, well-fed and completely at ease in the studiously elegant hotel dining room, with its antique mirrors, dazzling linens and hovering tuxedoed waiters.

I was still studying him when he looked up from the menu straight into my eyes, and smiled. It was a completely guileless smile, more of a grin really, and it transformed him from the self-satisfied middle-aged businessman I had imagined him into a boyish adventurer. I felt a rush of heat to my face and neck, as I allowed myself a small responding smirk, and then buried my nose self-consciously in the book I had brought with me.

I was beginning to entertain a harmless little fantasy - he would approach with an innocuous remark about the emptiness of the restaurant or the menu choices; we would chat, I'd invite him to join me at my table - when I felt a charge in the room. It was as if air was displaced or there was a sudden drop in temperature. I looked up. A woman was posing in the archway entrance to the dining room: a beautiful woman just beyond girlhood. She strode across the room with the lope of a runway model, and slid into the seat next to the man with the engaging smile. Now he turned its full wattage towards her, and my fantasy fizzled. He took her face between his hands and kissed her.

The woman's most notable feature was a mane of glossy black hair. It fell around her shoulders and obscured her face, until, with a dramatic gesture, she lifted it up with one hand and tossed it back. She was olive-skinned, Middle-Eastern perhaps, with large dark eyes outlined in kohl, and a wide mouth painted the Chanel Chinese Red currently in vogue. Her clothes were obviously expensive and sloppily worn, in a Prada-does-Catholic-schoolgirl style: white shirt with the collar up and cuffs unbuttoned, an oversized grey shrug, definitely cashmere, and an ultra-short pleated skirt in black and white plaid. The skirt revealed a long stretch of bare tanned leg leading to an unexpectedly masculine black leather lace-up boot, the kind that motorcyclists wear. The heavy footwear served to emphasize the fragility of her calf. She was tall and slim, probably taller than him, although she diplomatically hid the fact by hunching over to gaze upwards into his face as she draped her arms over his shoulders. They were the only other people in the hotel restaurant, and they couldn't keep their hands off each other.

They exchanged another long deep kiss, oblivious to the embarrassment of the waiter poised to take their order - or to mine, for that matter. They were in my direct line of vision. I toyed with the idea of moving my place setting to the side of the table to

4

turn myself ninety degrees away from the spectacle, but rejected it. I didn't want to draw attention to myself as a single woman dining alone, or to appear to be a prudish old maid. There was also a streak of stubbornness in my decision to stay put: I was here first; it was not my responsibility to accommodate their love-making; they should get themselves a room. In any event, I had, as usual when eating alone in restaurants, armed myself with a book, and I returned to it, as I waited for the arrival of my entrée.

I was back in London to mediate the separation of a Sixties rock icon and his partner of a dozen years. There were no children from the union, mercifully, but a lot of money rode on the quiet resolution of this affair, which had so far been lived in the public eye. The first session had gone extremely well, and I hoped that tomorrow's meeting would finalize the terms. In fact, I was so optimistic that I had confirmed my flight back home to Atlanta for the following day. I was already anticipating the pleasure of unlocking the front door of my little Craftsman bungalow, kicking off the heels and peeling off the pantyhose. I could then afford to cocoon for a couple of weeks, preparing for my next foray into the fraught world of high stakes disputes.

The restaurant book technique served two purposes: it slowed down my tendency to bolt my food as if there was a fire alarm sounding and this was my last meal on earth, a remnant no doubt of a childhood where mealtimes were unpredictable. It also slowed down the service. I've noticed that a woman dining alone is served at breakneck pace. The waiter no doubt expects that his tip, a percentage of the amount of the bill, will be meager, and is anticipating the free-spenders to come at a later seating. Even in this luxury establishment, and with a sparse Tuesday night clientele, I felt a little rushed. Besides, I was now intrigued by the amorous couple, and wanted to prolong my undercover observation. I turned a page, but wasn't reading.

Was she a trophy wife? I thought not. I had observed that this kind of overt passion rarely survived the wedding ceremony, and I couldn't see a ring. A high-priced hooker? Again, I decided against this explanation. In spite of the make-up and the short skirt, there was something refined about the girl. The ringless hand, for example, had short, clean, unpolished nails, not the stereotypical scarlet talons of a call girl. Perhaps, after all, they were just two people in love, in spite of the disparity in their ages. I was puzzled – and envious - about how she could stay so thin, and still attack her food with such obvious gusto. I hoped that this was not a prelude to a trip to the Ladies Room and self-induced regurgitation. On the other hand, her glass of champagne was hardly touched.

I returned to my Dover sole with leek puree. I had ordered the simplest thing on a menu crammed with "interesting" combinations. "Devonshire roast squab with a fig-anise coulis on a bed of julienned kohlrabi" was clearly the work of an ambitious chef, using the hotel kitchen to experiment with dishes he dreamed of serving one day in his own over-priced bistro. As a frequent business traveler, I had learned to beware of such experimental fare. I could not afford to be put off my game by a bout of indigestion. In any case, I was intent on maintaining my figure into my forties, a decade notorious for packing on the pounds. But I do love my food, and gave it – and a half-bottle of delicious Sancerre --all my attention, leaving my dinner companions to their own devices for a while.

When I had dealt with the fish, I leant back to sip my second glass of wine and resume my speculative study. The man was now talking quietly but emphatically on a cell phone. After a pause during which he was no doubt listening to the other party, he closed the apparatus decisively, and held the girl's eye for a long moment before he nodded. Her face broke into an expansive smile, she put her hands on either side of his head and pulled him to her for a smacking kiss on the lips. He beamed back at her.

This seemed the appropriate moment to call for the check, which arrived with almost magical speed. I wrote in my room number, added my signature and stood up. As I crossed the restaurant to the arch that separated it from the hotel lobby, I became aware of a disturbance ahead of me. A man was at the reception desk shouting and gesticulating. A tall person clothed in a burkah stood at his shoulder.

"I have a right to know! Tell me now, or I will—!"

The desk clerk remonstrated in lower tones. I could not make out his words. With what sounded like an oath, the man turned and came towards me, now shouting in a language I did not recognize, and followed by his shrouded companion. Our paths intersected at the entrance to the restaurant. The man lifted his arm and pointed at me, all the while keeping up his rant. My feet seemed leaden, as I struggled to make sense of the situation. It took a second before I understood that he was not looking at me but past me into the restaurant and at the only other diners there. At the same moment, I saw that the hand he was pointing was not empty, but contained a small black gun. I am at a loss to know what instinct drove me. Without thought, I launched my book - the only thing I had to hand. Last year's Booker prizewinner caught him square in the face at the same instant as the gun exploded. The man and I stared at each other in amazement. Then the burkah-clad figure set up a high-pitched keening, just as a burly security guard barreled into the gunman, knocking him to the ground, and sending the gun skittering across the marble floor.

I stood watching in a daze as another guard ran up to assist the first. Very quickly, police arrived, relieving the security guards who had pinned the assailant to the floor. The woman in the burkah – I assumed it was a woman, although I could not see her face through the dark mesh, and she uttered no sound other than

7

that unearthly wailing – was hurried away somewhere. After an uncertain passage of time, a policewoman came over to me.

"Are you all right?"

"Yes, I think so."

Silence, broken only by a metronomic tick. I looked down to find the source of the sound. At my feet, a garish spatter of scarlet marred the palely gleaming floor. As I watched, another drop splashed onto the marble.

"Just a minute! You're bleeding! Have you been shot?" I slowly raised my eyes to the young woman's face. What silly hats they make the English police wear, I thought. Shot? Why would she ask me that? Then I remembered the gun. But the man had been aiming back into the restaurant, not at me. I started to turn to see if the couple – my dining companions – were still there and unharmed, but the movement made me dizzy. It was as if the lighting had suddenly been turned down. I leant forward to peer into the gathering gloom of the restaurant. Somehow, I could not stop the leaning motion. The gloom turned to night, and I fell into it.

***

I came to in the ambulance, with the same policewoman crouched at my side.

"It's all right. The bullet just grazed your upper arm. The paramedic says you'll be right as rain, as soon as you've made up the loss of blood."

She turned for confirmation to a huge black man in surgical scrubs who was fiddling with an IV. He didn't take his eyes off the drip regulator, but nodded solemnly.

"Where am I going?"

"To Guy's Hospital. You're an American, aren't you? Well, Guy's is one of the best. Anyway, I'm sure you'll be out in no time. Just relax."

8

I was more than happy to comply, feeling too weak to frame any more questions. I lapsed into a doze as the ambulance screamed its way through the evening streets.

Her prediction proved correct. At the hospital, I was crisply cleaned, sutured and bandaged, and then left in a curtained-off cubicle to absorb another unit of IV fluid before being discharged into the London dawn with a supply of pain killers and instructions to see my own doctor as soon as I got home. I was in a taxi on the way back to my hotel before I registered that I had not been asked once for insurance details or even a credit card. The joys of socialized medicine! Before I left the hospital, however, I was asked to give a statement to the police. That was quickly done. No, I didn't know the assailant, the people he was presumably aiming at, or the woman in the burkah. I was literally caught in the crossfire, and could contribute nothing to help the inquiries.

My interrogator, a weasel-faced detective who replaced the pleasant young policewoman, was equally unable – or unwilling? – to provide me with answers to *my* questions. He would not tell me the identity of the gunman or his motive in coming to the hotel to attack one or both of the pair in the restaurant. He merely confirmed that the culprit was in custody, and that it was unlikely my testimony would be needed at trial in view of the several other witnesses on the scene.

As soon as I arrived back in my hotel room, I took two of the pain killers. While I waited for them to work their magic, I called to cancel my scheduled session with the rock star and his former lover, encouraging them to get together *without* their lawyers to capitalize on the progress made and close out any remaining details. I barely made it out of my wrinkled and probably irretrievably bloodstained dress before I collapsed into sleep.

When I woke, the midday sun was knifing through a gap in the drapes. My head was pounding, and my arm was throbbing.

I staggered to the bathroom to pee, and was on my way back to bed, determined to blank out the rest of the day with more drugs, when there was a knock at the door.

"A delivery for you!" The cheerful singsong set my teeth on edge, but I reached for one of the hotel's terrycloth robes and made myself decent before unlocking the door. I was confronted with an immense mass of white roses. There must have been four dozen at least. The flowers, which completely eclipsed their diminutive bearer, advanced into the room.

"On the desk, yes? Is your birthday?"

"Yes .... No .... Are you sure they're for me?"

"Sarah McKinney; Room 654, is right? You want I open the drapes?"

"Yes .... No ....." I sounded like a poorly trained parrot. I stood in the middle of the room staring perplexedly at the magnificent display, until I became conscious of the maid looking at me expectantly. I located my purse and struggled to find some pound coins in its depths.

"Thank you. Could you put the privacy notice on the door on your way out?"

Once alone, I advanced on the bouquet cautiously. Somewhere in its depths there should be a card telling me who the sender was. The perfume was heady, almost sickening in the overheated room. I extracted an envelope and retreated to sit on the bed before reading the card inside.

My dear Ms. McKinney,
Lelana and I are so distressed that you have been injured, but are eternally grateful for your courage in intervening on our behalf. We would like to express our thanks to you personally, and hope that you are sufficiently recovered to be our guest tonight. I will send a car at seven. My flat is close by and I promise you will be safely returned at an early hour.
Pieter Dykstra

There was a business card along with the card provided by the florist on which Pieter Dykstra had written his message: he was with "Europ News". No address, but a phone number and a website: www.europnews.co.uk. My immediate reaction was a mixture of resentment and curiosity. How presumptuous to arrange a car, as if I had no choice but to attend this command performance at a stranger's home! As far as I could remember, neither courage nor a wish to protect the couple in the restaurant had anything to do with my part in the events of the previous evening. Only an egomaniac would assume I was acting on his "behalf." On the other hand, I would like to know the rest of the story I had unwittingly been caught up in. What was the relationship between the middle-aged man with a Dutch name and the exotic beauty? Why were they the target of an enraged, gun-wielding foreigner and his traditionally-garbed accomplice? Despite their inappropriate public display of affection, there was something attractive about the couple. I had not decided to accept the invitation – summons was more accurate – but was leaning in that direction. At least, the business card had given me a foothold to research Dykstra's background. Meanwhile, I needed to check in again with my clients, and organize my travel plans accordingly. Strangely, my desire to crawl back under the covers had evaporated.

Chapter 2

Pieter Dykstra was waiting as the elevator door opened.

"Miss McKinney. I am so happy that you came! Welcome!"

"Please, call me Sarah."

He spoke with just a shade of an accent. I noted the way his heels came together and he bowed slightly, as I took his proffered hand. An Old World touch, very charming, and at odds with the stone-washed jeans and black T-shirt he was wearing. I felt uncomfortably overdressed in my charcoal grey pants suit, but the only casual outfit I had packed – a Donna Karan knit chemise that I bought a million years ago at a sample sale – was lying in the trash can in my hotel room, bloodstained and one sleeve ripped open to the shoulder.

His handshake was firm and warm. He stood aside, gesturing for me to precede him into the cramped entrance hall of his flat. It was, as he had said, not far from my hotel – a ten minute drive in the limousine he had sent – but located in an area of London unfamiliar to me. The car crossed to the South Bank at Charing Cross and then wound through twilit canyons between what used to be dockland warehouses, now converted into chic loft apartments, before arriving at a nondescript modern six-storey block. I had lived in London – on and off – as a child, but that had been in the late seventies before the industrial areas in the East End and south of the Thames had become fashionable. If any of those temporary lodgings had been in this neighborhood, I had successfully suppressed the memory.

The Indian driver got out to buzz me up. He had chatted pleasantly during the drive but was unable to fill in more details about my host than I had been able to glean from a quick Google search on my laptop back in the room. Dykstra was the London bureau chief of a news agency with offices in all the major European capitals. According to his bio on Europ News' website, he had been raised in Turkey and attended university in Germany. He spoke five languages.

"How is your arm? No pain, I hope?" He opened a door and ushered me through to the living room.

I was about to respond, but found myself unable to make a sound. To describe a view as breathtaking is cliché, but I honestly forgot to exhale for a second as I looked through the wall of glass facing me. The familiar dome of St. Paul's Cathedral dominated the skyline, outlined against a sky streaked in pink and gray. To the right, the steel and glass towers of the City reflected the setting sun. To the left glowed the pale arc of the Millennium footbridge and the creamy stone of Somerset House. And in the foreground, the Thames at high tide, its dark, oily surface bisected by the wake of a tourist boat making its last run down-river to Greenwich.

"Beautiful, isn't it? The view is the reason I took the flat. It's really very small, but you don't notice when you can see all this."

It says much about the view that I had not noticed Lelana until she uncoiled from a white leather sofa placed facing the windows. This time she had pulled her abundant hair into a loose chignon, with tendrils escaping to frame her face. She wore a silk tunic and leggings in a rich teal color. The outfit was reminiscent of traditional salwar, or Pakistani pajamas, but the cut was narrower and somehow suggested Parisian sophistication rather than Muslim modesty. Her feet were bare and I wore my four inch Manilos – one of my extravagances – yet she was a good three inches taller than me. As I took her hand – she just touched my fingers before withdrawing – I felt a stab of jealousy. However much I dieted, however much money I spent on designer clothes or how carefully I applied make-up, I would never be that tall, that young, that beautiful. Then I remembered that it was her, not me, who was the target of the murderous stranger the night before.

"May I give you a drink? Some wine perhaps? Lelana has prepared some food," Dykstra indicated the glass coffee table in front of the sofa on which there were three bowls of dips, each with its own artistically arranged fan of sliced fruit, vegetables and flat breads. My stomach reminded me I had barely eaten since the sole the night before.

"Just water for me. I'm taking meds that will send me straight to sleep if I drink alcohol."

"Some tea, then?"

"Yes, that would be lovely."

Lelana walked across to the breakfast bar that separated the kitchen from the living area, and assembled a tray for tea. The flat was indeed small. There was only one door other than the one I had entered. Presumably, that led to the bedroom and en suite bathroom. Besides the sofa and coffee table, there was really only space for one chair, an elegant modern recliner with a blond wood frame. Low bookcases lined two walls. I resisted the temptation to browse the titles; most looked serious, biographies or current events. No art work, no television or computer. If you could ignore the view, which was close to impossible – even if I turned my back to it, I felt it looming there - the apartment felt anonymous, like a room hastily assembled for a photo shoot.

After I had been settled with a glass of fragrant green-tinged tea, and invited to sample the various hors d'oeuvres, I turned to Dykstra with the question I had been rehearsing since I received his invitation.

"Can you tell me what that was all about last night?"

He sighed and took a sip of his wine before responding.

"Again, I am so sorry that you were hurt. So unfortunate ….. It's not a complicated story. Let me explain some background. Lelana was born in Jordan of Lebanese parents – a very wealthy family. They moved to Amman when civil war broke out in Beirut in the sixties. Lelana was educated in Switzerland, and then came to London to study art history. Last year, her father summoned her back home. She found out when she got to Amman that he had arranged a marriage for her. Her fiancé is older, much older, and …. *not* a nice man. He is a fundamentalist, very traditional. If she marries him, she will never be allowed any freedom. She will have to give up her studies. She won't even be allowed to drive."

I sneaked a look sideways at Lelana, sitting next to me on the couch. This was *her* story. Why wasn't *she* telling it? She sat with her legs curled gracefully under her, her eyes downcast, as demure as any traditional husband-to-be could wish. Maybe her lack of English held her back from speaking. Unlikely, given the education Dykstra had described. Then, after all, *he* was the reporter, with the better skill for narrative. I turned back to Dykstra.

"And how did you and Lelana get to know each other?"

"I was in Jordan in May working on a story. A friend of Lelana's approached me and asked if I would help her. Help her escape, she meant; help her get to London and start a new life. We met at the friend's home – it all had to be secret. So, here we are." He looked over at Lelana with – what? Love? Lust?

I had spent many hundreds of hours in mediation learning to read the subtle clues people reveal when they tell their story. Even when the tale has been well-rehearsed, even when the party relies on his or her attorney to voice it, there is usually a little tic, subtle body language that shows when someone is shading the truth, hiding something, or misrepresenting their true feelings. Dykstra was a hard read. He spoke confidently, and made good eye contact. Even across the restaurant the night before I was forced to acknowledge his charm. Now, I felt the warmth of his attraction at close quarters. And yet there was something "off," some indefinable resistance in my response to the romantic story he was recounting. I concluded that my hesitation came from Lelana's silence, and I determined to include her in the conversation.

"Couldn't you have spoken to your father? Persuaded him that you didn't want to marry this man?" I addressed Lelana directly, willing her to look at me, but, although she responded, she kept her eyes on her hands in her lap.

"After my mother died, my father changed. My aunt, his sister, took over the household. She is a very strict Muslim. She made my father change. I can't talk to him now."

"And that man last night, the one who shot me?"

Dykstra took over again.

"A thug hired by the fiancé. It was supposed to be an "honor" killing! Pah! His so-called honor is hurt because she ran away, so he hires someone to murder her."

"Is that what the police say? What about the woman with him? Who is she?"

I saw Lelana stiffen. I guessed she knew the woman, but she didn't speak.

"The police know nothing, and they will do nothing! The authorities will be happy to deport the man to avoid any unpleasantness with Middle-Eastern allies. There will be nothing in the papers. It will all be hushed up." Dykstra sounded disgusted but resigned.

I pointed out that he was a journalist. Surely he could expose the attempted murder and the reason for it, and engage the public on Lelana's behalf. For the first time, I saw the briefest indication that he was uncomfortable. His eyes moved to the view over the river, and he buried his nose in his wine glass before answering.

"Ah, yes. That is the dilemma. If I was just a journalist, I would do as you say. But I am also Lelana's lover, her protector, her only friend here. I cannot allow her privacy to be invaded, her life story to be paraded for millions to read, her photo to be gloated over." He broke off, with a shrug. "Anyway, we think she is safe. We are on guard now. They won't try again, having failed so badly..."

I thought his confidence in Lelana's safety was a bit glib, but I didn't comment. I allowed him to lead the conversation into other areas. He asked questions about my work, intelligent and well-phrased questions that demonstrated his journalistic skills, but all with a charm that diffused any feeling that I was being interviewed. We talked about America. He had traveled widely in the U.S. and was better informed on many of the political issues of the day than most Americans. I described Atlanta, the "city too busy to hate," the northside sprawl of shopping centers and traffic-clogged parkways, and the quiet little in-town neighborhoods like mine, transformed each spring by dogwoods and azaleas into extravagant wedding chapels of pink and white blossoms.

Lelana said little, but followed the talk, smiling quietly, and making sure my glass was refilled with tea. She seemed a different person than the exuberant young woman in the restaurant the evening before. Perhaps her brush with violence had subdued her, or perhaps this was her normal domestic side, comfortable with letting others talk while she looked after their creature comforts. There was only one discordant moment. Lelana was going to get more tea. As she passed behind Dykstra's chair, she trailed her finger tips across the back of his neck. He leant into her caress, but she was not looking at him. She was looking directly at me with narrowed eyes and her mouth in a straight line. The challenge was clear: stay away, this man is mine. The moment passed, and when she returned to fill my glass, her face was again arranged in a calm smile.

17

Talking about home reminded me that I had an early flight the next day, and I began to prepare my exit, thanking them for a lovely evening, and again admiring the glorious view which, while we had been talking, had transformed into a light show, with the cityscape silhouetted against the night sky.

Dykstra telephoned for the car.

"It will be here in five minutes. Oh, I almost forgot! We have a gift for you to show our gratitude." Waving off my polite demurrers that it really wasn't necessary, he disappeared into the bedroom, and came out a few seconds later with a cardboard box about eight inches cubed. He placed it on the coffee table in front of me and gestured for me to open it.

"It's ….. beautiful." I held in my hands a small bronze sphinx, the mythical animal with the body of a lion and the head of a woman, familiar from the massive ruins in the Egyptian desert. This one weighed about three pounds. It was delicately cast, the implacable stare highlighted by lines etched around the eyes. I thought immediately of Lelana's eye make-up the night before. There was even a resemblance in the statuette's mouth, full lips curved into a slight smile.

"I can't accept this – it's really too much." I suspected that this kind of fine craftsmanship did not come cheap. I was nervous about transporting an expensive piece of art, perhaps one of historical significance, through customs.

"We insist you accept it. It is a very small way to repay you for your courage."

"Well, it *is* so lovely …… Thank you both very much. Um, I will need to declare this on the customs form tomorrow. How should I describe it?" This was the most delicate way I could think of to obtain the information I would need: the statue's value.

"Please don't worry. You can find this kind of piece in the bazaars throughout the Middle East. It's craftsman's work, not mass-produced, but not expensive." A fellow frequent traveler, he had read my mind. "Put 'small bronze figure, value $50.'"

Through this exchange I was aware of Lelana at my shoulder. Her tension, from the moment Dykstra emerged with the box, was singing like electricity in the room. *She didn't want him to give me the statue.* I turned towards her, but as if she sensed my flash of intuition, she quickly bent away to gather the tea glasses. I hesitated, unsure of whether to confront her with my suspicion that the little sphinx was somehow too precious to hand off to a near stranger. It would be extremely bad manners to question her about it, especially as I had already accepted the gift. Did Dykstra sense her reluctance too? He seemed oblivious, as he moved to answer the entry phone.

"The car's here. I do hope we meet again. Please don't hesitate to contact me if I can be of help in any way. You have my e-mail address, and I have yours." I had given him my business card earlier, when we had discussed the possibility of an article about international dispute resolution.

My opportunity to probe Lelana was gone. With his hand under my elbow, Dykstra was escorting me to the elevator, repeating his appreciative phrases and promises of future service. I made a last effort as we stood by the elevator. The door to the apartment was closed with Lelana inside.

"Is Lelana allright with –"

He broke in, speaking urgently in a hushed voice.

"She's upset, very nervous, but won't speak about it. She refuses to leave the flat, and wants me to stay with her. All I can do is try and be confident and calm, and hope that she will follow my lead. I must go back to work at some point. I hope the shock of the attack will wear off in time. That's why I was so glad you agreed to come – so she could see a strong woman coping with grace."

I was embarrassed to find myself blushing. I have schooled myself to be immune to flattery. There are always a few parties, or more usually their attorneys, who think that the neutral can be swayed. But I could not deny my attraction to this man with his vigorous good looks and old-fashioned courtesies. Besides, he had unerringly found my Achilles heel: my pride in being a strong, independent person, not easily put off her stroke by the unexpected. I stammered something as the elevator doors opened, and I stepped in.

As the doors moved together, Dykstra remained standing there smiling, his head slightly inclined forward. I will never see him again, I told myself as the elevator descended. No point in giving him, or his mysterious girlfriend, another thought. Tomorrow, it's back to the real world.

Chapter 3

I love my house.

Buying it ten years ago when I returned to Atlanta after five frustrating years in New York City was an act of faith. I was determined to start a mediation practice, but had little beyond a few law school contacts and a conviction that there had to be a better way to resolve disputes than submit them to twelve bored and probably biased citizens. The house took all my savings and a lot of my time over the first few years, which proved to be a godsend. Ripping up brown shag carpeting to reveal heart-of-pine planks beneath, chipping off several layers of toxic lead paint from sash windows that hadn't been opened in fifty years, then working out how to replace the broken cords, all built a deeper and more sustaining relationship than with any of the lovers I've shared my life with. When my caseload was non-existent and I was sorely tempted by a regular paycheck (with bonus) dangled by Atlanta law firms dazzled by my law school grades and big city resume, I strapped on my tool belt and tackled a new DIY challenge. The good ol' boys at the Home Depot on Lawrenceville Highway were my best friends, and my house was my creative outlet, my biggest investment, and my refuge.

Now, tugging my carry-on bag over the tree roots that erupted through the sidewalk, I contemplated the changes in the neighborhood since I moved in. Then, it was all I could afford, but over the last few years, house prices had soared, spurred by the extension of the MARTA light rail system. Most of my neighbors, young professionals, had pushed up through the attic to add an extra floor, or knocked down the back wall to create a gourmet kitchen. Mine was about the only bungalow on the street that remained as nature – and the 1911 Sears Roebuck catalog – intended. Filtered through the leaves of the massive water oaks that lined the street, the September afternoon sun dappled the front porch, and my jet-lagged heart swelled with pride.

I have a routine for returning from business trips. I drop the suitcase inside the front door and kick off my shoes. Then, undressing as I go, I head for the bedroom to put on sweat pants and T-shirt. I head back through the living room to the kitchen, put the kettle on for tea, and open the back door to check out the backyard. Only after I have taken a few sips of tea, and browsed through the accumulated mail, do I start to unpack.

I had buried the bronze statuette in the middle of my dirty clothes, dispensing with the cardboard box it came in. I pulled it out and looked hard into the sphinx's eyes. What was the old story? Those that could not answer her riddle, she devoured alive. But I had a riddle for *her*: who were Dykstra and Lelana really? Were they merely lovers or conspirators? Was the attack that wounded me an attempted honor killing, as Dykstra claimed, or something darker, more complex? The sphinx smiled back, inscrutable and beautiful. I sighed, and looked around for a place to put her. The center of the dining table seemed best for the time being. I set her down, and turned my attention to fixing something to eat before tiredness overtook me.

The next day was Friday. Most of it was spent in the tedious but essential paperwork that follows a case. I made some phone calls, dealt with emails, and started up the process for the next mediation. I remembered to call and make an appointment with my doctor to check the bullet wound in my arm, as instructed by the emergency room doctor in London. The first available time was Monday. I thought about seeing if there was a movie I might like to go to, but by eight o'clock I was already exhausted. I slept late on Saturday, then did some serious grocery shopping. The rest of the weekend spun by, occupied with chores around the house and yard, and a handful of other errands in Decatur. The weather was perfect; all the heat and humidity of summer had dissipated while I was in London, and it was a pleasure to be outside. I even squeezed in a run, although I was disgusted to find myself gasping after a couple of miles.

I managed not to think about Dykstra, at least not much. When I did, Lelana was a shadow at his shoulder. I could not separate the two, even though they posed separate puzzles. I was attracted to him in a way I had not been attracted to anyone for years. I wanted to trust him, but was wary of his charm. Lelana, I did not trust. She changed personalities like clothes. I didn't understand her agenda, but it seemed clear that she certainly had one. I speculated about their relationship. They were lovers, certainly, but were they *in* love? An intense sexual affair seemed more believable, fueled perhaps on her side by gratitude to him for having rescued her. I didn't need to guess at what drove Dykstra into bed with her.

***

About eleven on Monday morning, I got home from the doctor's. She said the wound was healing nicely, and the stitches would dissolve in a couple more days. We chatted, me filling her in on the events that led to me being shot, but I was in and out in twenty minutes. I pulled the Honda up to the garage, a separate building at the back of my property, and hefted the dry-cleaning I had collected on the way home. I was halfway to the back door when I sensed that something was wrong. It took me a few more steps before I pinpointed what it was. One of the three glass panes set side by side in the top of the door - the pane closest to the lock --was missing. A space about eight inches wide and sixteen inches

23

high yawned black. A tall person, or a short one standing on something, could easily reach through to the inside, release the deadbolt and open the door.

With the realization that the intruder might still be in the house, I froze, then tiptoed awkwardly back to the driveway. I crept around the side of the house, glancing quickly into the bedroom and office windows – nothing out of order - then, dumping the dry-cleaning next to the mailbox, I hurried behind one of the oak trees and pulled out my cell phone.

"Police ...... I want to report a break-in, they may still be inside." I gave the address and my name, and was told – redundantly – to stay where I was and not try to enter the house. While I waited, I contemplated the neighborhood. The houses were silent. Their occupants were busy at their downtown offices at this hour. If they had children, they were at school. It was extremely unlikely anyone had seen an intruder.

Within ten minutes, a blue-and-white Decatur police patrol car pulled up, without siren or flashing lights, and two uniformed policemen got out. One, the driver, was ridiculously young; the other was a middle-aged woman. The young one approached me.

"Ms. McKinney? I'm Officer Johnson, and this is Officer Terry. Have you seen any movement from the house?"

"No. I guess they've gone."

"OK," He turned to his partner, "I'll take the back and you wanna go in the front? Could we have your door keys, please."

I handed them over, and watched the one called Johnson sprint up the driveway and disappear behind the house. Officer Terry took her time to heave herself up the front steps, and fiddle with the front door lock, before she too disappeared from view. Two minutes later, they emerged together on the porch and signaled me over.

"No one inside, but someone definitely broke in through the back door. Come and tell us what's missing."

I was braced for a scene of chaos: furniture overturned, contents of cupboards and drawers spilled. But the living room was as neat as I had left it a couple of hours before, Bose sound system still in place. I rushed through to the second bedroom that I used as my office. Thank God, the laptop computer was there undisturbed on the desk – it contained all my work files and client data – together with the printer and a few hard copy files I was working on. Next, I went into the bedroom, the younger male cop a pace behind me. I keep $250 in emergency cash in the top drawer of my bureau, along with a little leather covered box that contains the few pieces of good jewelry I possess. All present and correct.

"I can't see that anything is missing."

"Sometimes it's kids after prescription drugs or alcohol."

I led the way to the bathroom and opened the medicine cabinet. My bottle of Ambien and the container with the four Vicodin left from the supply I received at Guy's Hospital in London were still there, along with some over-the-counter remedies. In the kitchen, my bottle of vodka remained in the freezer compartment and the countertop wine rack still held five bottles of my favorite Central Coast Cabernet. We returned to the living room where Officer Terry was seated at my dining table, laboriously filling in a report form.

"Perhaps they got the wrong house." I offered weakly. Johnson shrugged. Without looking up, his partner said "So, nothing taken; no property damage other than pane of glass removed from door." She put away his pen, yawned ostentatiously, and pushed herself up to standing.

"Wait! Yes, there's something …. There was a statue on the table. It's gone. I didn't notice before, because I've only had it a few days, and I'm not used to seeing it there."

Officer Terry looked put out at having to revise her report, but the other cop seemed interested.

"Is it valuable? Can you describe it for us?"

"I was told it was worth about $50." His face fell. I described it in as much detail as I could, although it didn't seem that many of the details were transcribed into the report. I saw that his partner was having a difficult time with "sphinx", finally crossing the word out and printing "statue" instead.

"So, what happens now? Will someone come to dust for fingerprints?" Officer Terry, already at the door, smirked, leaving it to her partner to explain with an embarrassed giggle.

"Um, I'm afraid we're not CSI. We just don't have the resources. Burglary, at least when there's nobody hurt and no real property damage, it's low priority. We'll put the word out about the, er, sphinx. It may turn up at a pawn shop or flea market. You can check back with us."

He handed me a card. "You should get that door fixed as soon as possible. And you might want to change the locks."

"Why? Whoever broke in didn't have a key."

"Well, it's just that … we say that because … it usually makes the homeowner feel more secure, you know …" He looked even more embarrassed.

Yeah, and makes money for your buddy the locksmith, I thought. When did I become so cynical? This officer was now as eager to leave as the other. Did they pair them up deliberately: good cop, bad cop?

After they left, I sat down in the chair recently vacated by the policewoman, and stared over clenched fists at the phantom oblong in the center of the table where the sphinx had so briefly rested . From the moment I had spotted the missing pane of glass until now, I had marched forward, thinking it through, taking practical steps, problem solving in the same logical fashion as I advised my clients to do. Now, alone, I felt a visceral reaction. My whole body began to quiver and I felt a weight on my chest that turned my breath shallow and rapid. Some stranger had been here in this room, had looked around at – perhaps touched -- my things. On the nightly news, they've taken to calling break-ins "home invasions." That was exactly what it felt like: an invasion. My sanctuary had been penetrated.

I concentrated on my breathing. In a minute or less, the panic ebbed, as it always does. A few years ago, I had seen a therapist about these attacks. She had wanted to trawl for the roots of my anxiety in the troubled waters of my childhood, when I was Sally Ann dressed in thrift store clothes, not Sarah who shopped at Saks Fifth Avenue. I had declined to cooperate, and so she had gracefully switched tracks to give me some biofeedback tools for handling my symptoms: breathing, mantras, meditation. Whether these techniques worked, or the attacks merely ran their course, I don't know, but I employed them dutifully on the rare occasions I needed to. This had been my first recurrence in nearly a year.

When I felt up to it, I went back through the kitchen to pick up the broken glass. It lay in several large pieces. I carefully wrapped them in cardboard, before thoroughly sweeping the whole area for any tiny shards that might have escaped notice. Replacing the pane of glass was a task I would normally take care of myself. Measuring, cleaning out the surround, selecting the right putty, the job was well within my expertise and one I might have otherwise enjoyed. But I wanted it done fast.

I called Gerardo, a handyman who had helped me with some of the projects that needed four hands or a sturdier back than mine. I had met Gerardo and his lovely wife Serafina when I volunteered as a teacher at an English for immigrants class. My travel schedule prevented me from continuing to teach a regular class, but the couple had impressed me with their eagerness to learn, even after a long day at work, and even when Serafina was heavily pregnant. When I ran into Gerardo in the parking lot at

Home Depot some time later, I had been happy to take his proudly offered business card announcing that "Gerry" could help with all building projects, had reasonable rates and was reliable. And, reliably, he said he would be there at eight the following morning.

I duct-taped a piece of plywood over the gap in the door, and found a broom handle to wedge against it: all I could do to defend my castle for now.

As I worked, I argued with myself. The moment I realized that the sphinx – and *only* the sphinx – had been taken, I had the impulse to call Dykstra. My rational, independent self was fighting that urge. I didn't need to get mixed up in whatever or whoever linked Dykstra and Lelana to a high-end tourist souvenir that someone wanted enough to follow across the Atlantic. The police had made it clear the burglar would not be caught. Let him have the statue. Once the door was fixed, I need not think about the whole affair ever again.

And yet …… It wasn't just curiosity that drove me to pick up the phone. Yes, I was intrigued and wanted answers, but underlying that – my *real* motive - was a desire for contact with Dykstra. Telling him about the theft was an excuse to hear his voice again.

When he answered, that voice sounded urgent and strangely intimate over the thousands of miles.

"Hello?"

"Hi, it's Sarah McKinney. I'm sorry to bother you, but something—"

"Sarah! I thought for a moment … Lelana! She's gone! She's disappeared!"

Chapter 4

Telephoning Dykstra was a major step out of character for me, or at least the me I thought I had created painstakingly over the years: cool, dispassionate, independent, an observer of human nature. In my relationships with men – my prior relationships, that is – I always retained the upper hand, measuring my feelings to ensure that when the affair ended, I was able to walk away unscathed. I had never ever pursued a man who was already taken. Against my better judgment, I was not only reaching out to a man who was living with another woman, but a man embroiled in some kind of mystery involving criminal violence and theft. I should have cut the call off immediately. I didn't.

"What happened?" I asked.

"I went into work about noon. I've been staying home with Lelana, but there were things I needed to see to. When I got back, she was gone."

"Were there signs of a struggle?"

"No ……. Some clothes were gone, jewelry, her passport ….." Dykstra's voice faded as the implications hung between us. This was no abduction then; more like a stealthily planned escape. I couldn't help feeling a pleasant little skip in my chest: Lelana had left him. He had served his purpose in enabling her escape from a repugnant arranged marriage, and she was ready to spread her wings with a more age-appropriate crowd. However, I was careful to pretend there might be another explanation.

"Did you call the police?"

"They won't accept a "missing person" report until 24 hours have passed. They say she's probably gone shopping!"

"Well, maybe ....." After a second or two, I returned to the supposed reason for my call. "Something odd has happened. I wonder if it might be linked to Lelana's disappearance, although I don't see how. The little sphinx, the statue you gave me, it's been stolen. Someone broke into my house this morning and took it. Nothing else, just the sphinx. Could it be more valuable than you think? I, er, I thought Lelana seemed upset about you giving it to me. I might have imagined it, of course, just an impression I had."

"The statue? No, I bought it in Cairo before I even met Lelana. And I assure you, it isn't an historic artifact, or anything valuable. I can't imagine why it was stolen, unless the thief thought it looked like it was worth something. Perhaps Lelana was surprised when I gave it to you. I didn't tell her I was going to, but after all it was mine and there was no reason to get her approval. She didn't say anything to me about it after you left. "

"Well, don't worry about it, then. The police seem to think it's unlikely to be found. Burglaries are a low priority for them." I repeated drily the line the police had given me an hour or so earlier.

"I am so sorry. We – I – seem to have brought you nothing but bad luck: the shooting, now a break-in. You will wish you had never met me!" He laughed briefly.

"No, I don't wish that at all. I just hope we can get to know each other without any more drama." I was blushing, and furious with myself for doing so, but at least he couldn't see me.

His voice softened. "Sarah, yes, I hope for that too." He paused, and I searched for something to prolong the conversation, but we had both said enough for now. "May I telephone you tomorrow? Just to check in? No more drama, I promise."

"Yes, please, I'd like that." I put the phone down carefully, then allowed myself a little victory dance around the sofa. Yes! Lelana had left him and he was going to call me tomorrow. That night, I slept much better than I deserved to, considering the lingering ache in my bicep as the gunshot wound healed, and that my back door still bore the scars of a recent break-in.

***

Gerardo arrived at eight, took measurements, and left to get the glass and other supplies he would need to fix the back door. I had brought back a Peter Rabbit soft toy from the Harrods' duty-free shop at Heathrow for his two-year old son Javier. Gerardo accepted it almost gruffly, but I didn't mind. Over time, Gerardo and I had evolved a relationship at once distant and affectionate. We respected each other's skills, and worked together like comrades, sweating in the crawl space to locate a recalcitrant electric cable, or me spotting for him as he spread-eagled across the roof shingles in search of a leak.

Sometimes, in good weather, and when the project was outside, Serafina and Javier came with him. The first time, it had taken much urging on my part to get them out of the truck, Serafina insisting that they were fine, "Please, no problem!" even though the sun was beating down on the metal cab. I spread a blanket under the oak tree, and hunted out some shoe boxes and tissue paper – all I had on hand that might serve as suitable toys. Before long, Javier was staggering around the yard, in that delightful bow-legged gait that toddlers have, picking up stones and leaves and bringing them to Serafina, a shy Madonna sitting in the center of the blanket, her skirt spread over outstretched legs to catch her son's offerings. I grew to like having them there, and was vaguely disappointed when Gerardo came alone. My *ersatz* family. I scolded myself for my sentimentality. After all, I had never been

31

invited to their house, and didn't expect to be. I operated on the "don't ask, don't tell" principle with regard to his immigration status. Our conversations were mainly conducted in monosyllables.

I was on my second cup of coffee when he came through to the living room to say he had finished. I inspected the newly glazed pane. Gerardo had cleaned up the putty on the other two panes so that the new work did not stand out.

"Perfect! How much do I owe you?"

I led the way back to the living room, Gerardo cleaning his hands off on a rag as he followed.

"Sarah, is a car. There at eight when I come. And when I come from Home Depot is always there. Two people ..." He pointed to his eyes and then at me.

"Two people in a car watching me? Watching the house?"

"*Si.* Maybe nothing ......"

"Show me." I walked out onto the front porch with Gerardo close behind. I bent over the porch rail as if to show him something. "What kind of car?"

"White Toyota Camry." Gerardo may not have mastered the past tense in English, but his knowledge of cars was pluperfect. The car was parked on the other side of the street, one house down. Because of the angle, I could not see the faces of the two occupants, only their upper torsos.

"OK. Let's go back inside." I went in search of my check book, wondering what to do. I could always call the police. I had Officer Johnson's card. I suspected that a car parked legally on a suburban street would be even lower priority than a break-in, so I quickly dismissed the idea.

"Do you have other work this morning, Gerardo?" I indicated my watch. "Do you have some more time for me?"

"*Si!*" He grinned. "No work. What you want I do?"

I added $50 to the total on the invoice he had given me, signed the check, and straightened up. Gerardo was not tall, but he was broad-shouldered, and years of construction work had given him the weather-beaten look, as well as the scars, of a veteran fighter. I was warmed by the thought that, if I had asked, he would have confronted the watchers on my behalf then and there, but I wasn't going to risk his deportation on a possible assault charge.

"I'd like you to leave in your truck, but park around the corner and come back on foot, in case those people in the car are waiting for you to go before they come into the house. It's probably nothing, but – " I waved vaguely towards the back door he had just repaired, "the break-in makes me nervous."

I think both of us were more excited than nervous.

Within a few minutes of Gerardo's truck making its noisy exit from my driveway, there was a knock at the front door. Through the front window, I was taken aback to see Lelana standing on the front porch, her shoulders hunched. She must have gone directly to the airport after Dykstra left his flat yesterday at noon, and caught the last plane out. I backed away quickly from the window before she saw me, and then stood, trying to figure out why on earth she should run out on Dykstra and then come to see me. There was only one way to find out. I opened the door, but not wide enough to invite her in. Instead, I stepped out onto the porch to greet her.

"Lelana! What brings you to the U.S.?"

"You are surprised, no? I thought, Atlanta, that is Sarah's home. I will visit to see if her arm is better." She smiled widely, but her eyes flicked around tensely, and I could see the outline of her hands clenching into fists in the pockets of the little poplin jacket she was wearing. Today, she was back in casual fashionista mode: her luxuriant raven hair loose and tousled, a pair of ultra-skinny jeans, and the motorcycle boots I recognized from the restaurant where I had first seen her. But there was none of the self-assurance she had displayed that night, or at Dykstra's flat. She was unable to hide her nervousness.

My level gaze must have signaled to her that I wasn't buying the friendly "I was in the neighborhood" line. I decided to play my cards close to my chest.

"How did you get here?"

She gestured vaguely over her shoulder. "A cab dropped me off. I will call for pick-up."

Another lie. The white Toyota Camry was parked across the street, although now there was just one person visible inside.

"Beautiful house. Can I see inside?"

I debated whether to let her in. It seemed churlish to keep her out on the porch. I opened the front door reluctantly, and gestured for her to enter.

She walked to the center of the living room.

"Lovely …" Her eyes scanned every surface. "May I have a glass of water?"

She wanted me out of sight in the kitchen, so she could explore further. I wasn't going to play her game.

"O.K., Lelana. Why are you here, really?"

She feigned shock, then appeared to calculate. Another false smile.

"Listen, I came to get the statue. The sphinx that Pieter gave you? It was a mistake. The statue belongs to me. He should not have given it to you. It's very important to me."

"Why?"

"Why?" Her eyes searched every corner of the room before she answered. "My mother gave it to me. My dead mother ….."

She seemed genuinely upset. Who should I believe, Dykstra or her? It didn't matter: I didn't have what she wanted.

"I don't have the statue, Lelana. Someone stole it from me. It's not here."

Now, her shock was definitely real. "What do you mean? Where is it? I must have it!"

"I don't know. It's gone."

A raucous squeal invaded the room, the sound of machinery revved high. I rushed to the front door, Lelana behind me. Gerardo was standing at the bottom of the steps to the front porch, facing along the path to the driveway. He had protective goggles on, and heavy gauntleted work gloves. A chainsaw juddered and kicked in his hands. Facing him, at the driveway end of the path, was a tall, muscular stranger. His head was shaved smooth. He was wearing a pale gray suit with a slight sheen, and a black shirt open at the neck: gangster clothes, I thought. In a swarthy face, his eyes gleamed strangely pale. His mouth carved a straight line across black stubble. The two men faced off like gunslingers in an old western.

Lelana ran to the porch rail and shouted something, but over the racket of the chainsaw, the stranger could not have heard her. He began to move up the path. Lelana darted past me and down the steps. She edged around Gerardo, who never took his eyes off the other man or his hand off the chain saw's throttle. When she reached the man, she grabbed his arm and shouted furiously in his ear. She appeared to be trying to drag him away. At least he stopped advancing. The stand-off continued: Gerardo repeatedly gunning the chainsaw, Lelana imploring the man to leave, the thug maintaining his threatening stance. I felt like I was watching a low-budget movie. Then, without warning, the man shrugged off Lelana's grip and turned away. As he strode down the driveway, Lelana scurrying behind, Gerardo killed the chain saw motor. The sudden silence rang in my ears. It was punctuated by the slam of one car door, then another. The Camry left with a screech of rubber on asphalt.

Gerardo expelled air with an audible "phew". He put the chainsaw carefully down on the path, pulled the goggles down so they hung around his neck, and slowly climbed the porch steps, peeling off his work gloves as he approached.

"Friends from work?" This was a phrase from Unit 1 of "Practical English for Immigrants." We had drilled the model conversation repeatedly when I taught the ESL class. It came back to me now, and I couldn't help responding.

"Yes, this is Rosita and this is Ling Lee."

A bubble of hysterical laughter escaped me. A moment later, we were both doubled over on the porch, hands on knees, tears running down our faces. When we recovered, I led the way back inside.

"Do you want a beer?"

Chapter 5

Although I kept beer in the refrigerator for guests, I rarely drank it. It had a peculiar effect on me: it made me crave dark chocolate.

After Gerardo left, I spent a frantic ten minutes searching for the bar I had hidden from myself weeks before. I eventually found it in a kitchen drawer, nestled between the aluminum foil and the Saran wrap. I retreated to the sofa, where I stretched out with the unwrapped chocolate bar lying on my stomach. I broke off a square and popped it into my mouth. Wickedly delicious. I ate another square.

I was feeling restless, and decidedly disinclined to work. My next scheduled mediation was in New York in three weeks. There were briefs to read, law and other background research to tackle. I prided myself on entering the mediation room better prepared than anyone else there, but right now I could not bear the thought of sitting in front of a computer screen. Instead, I reflected on the events of the last week, picking each one up carefully like a rock and looking for new perceptions to scurry out from underneath like woodlice. The shooting, for example: was the keening woman in the burkah Lelana's aunt? But perhaps that story about her walking out on an arranged marriage was a fiction, and the shooter had been aiming for Dykstra. Investigative journalists lead dangerous lives, especially when they expose truths that powerful people want to hide. And how to explain the change in Lelana's demeanor between the restaurant and Dykstra's apartment the next day? It could have been shock in the aftermath of the attack; that was Dykstra's explanation. But the whole dynamic of her relationship with Dykstra seemed to have changed overnight. Then I considered yesterday's break-in. Either Dykstra or Lelana must have told someone I had the sphinx. No one else, except a bored customs officer at Atlanta Hartsfield Airport, knew I had brought it home with me from London. If it was Lelana, she could not have known that the person she told would arrange for its recovery, or else why did she come looking for it herself? The sphinx was important; it held the key.

Finally, I turned my thoughts, almost reluctantly, to Pieter Dykstra. Was this fascination with him just a symptom of my restlessness? Had I become too comfortable and settled in my ways, and was this possible *liaison dangereuse* just a way to shake myself up with a new challenge? Realistically, with Dykstra in London and me in Atlanta, there was no future to our relationship, if it could be dignified with that label. After all, we had shared nothing more than appraising glances in the restaurant that first night, and a pleasant-enough evening in the company of his girlfriend. The most intimacy we had exchanged was a handshake that lasted a second or two longer than strictly appropriate. Until yesterday. In our phone conversation, it had been me who had pushed the point with uncharacteristic forwardness. His response, now I reflected on it, was no more than polite. I knew next to nothing about him or his feelings. If I was looking for a new challenge, I'd be better off training for a marathon. Running after Pieter Dykstra was likely to prove a fruitless exercise.

***

Since my twelfth birthday when I ran away from the chaos that I still refused to call "home," into the stiffly bureaucratic arms of the London Borough of Wandsworth's Social Services Department, I had been running in one way or another all my life. Back then, I had been lucky to be fostered with Margaret

Mumford, a spinsterish high school English teacher, but I never relaxed my efforts to distance myself from my past. I threw myself into geekdom, studying harder and longer than any other pupil at the Clapham Abbey School for Girls, Miss Mumford's employer, from whose aristocratic but well-meaning Board she had wrestled a scholarship for me. I worked not only to make up for learning time lost during my nomadic childhood, but to acquire a protective disguise that would excuse me from pressure to be one of the cool girls, the ones with the super-cool boyfriends, a competition for which I had neither the wardrobe nor the social skills.

"Knowledge itself is power. That is all ye know on earth, and all ye need to know."

Miss Mumford didn't need to raise her voice to get attention. Barely five foot tall, with bird-like delicacy, she could quell a class of exuberant teenage girls with a regal lift of the chin and a piercing look from her clear dark eyes. Her white hair was cut short as a man's and she favored navy blue or dark grey skirts to mid-calf topped with unfashionable pastel twin-sets, as if stuck in an English country house mystery in the role of the impecunious maiden aunt.

"Miss M., you've muddled quotations."

"Very good, Sally Ann." This was in the days before I reinvented myself as Sarah. "Yes, Francis Bacon and John Keats make strange bedfellows, but the totality serves a greater truth. And …?"

I would roll my eyes and sigh exaggeratedly as only a fourteen-year-old can, before supplying the start of the Keats quote.

"Beauty is truth; truth, beauty."

I pretended to be embarrassed and bored by Miss Mumford's literary games, but in fact I loved our sparring. I lived with her for four years during which she cut her way through a maze of red tape that separated me from my birthright, an

American passport. In the course of that heroic struggle, she unearthed a legacy from a great aunt who had known of my existence while I had been completely ignorant of hers. That legacy, dedicated to "educational purposes" funded my move to Georgia and my undergraduate education at Rome College, a small liberal arts school in the foothills of the Appalachians. I wished I could call Miss Mumford up now, and get her take on all this, but she was forever "number unobtainable" beneath six feet of earth and a plain granite slab in the Central Wandsworth Cemetery.

I was a second year associate with a three-hundred lawyer Wall Street firm when I learned she had died. I'm ashamed to say that I was initially reluctant to spare the time to go to the funeral. I was buried neck deep in documents for a big anti-trust case. It was boring work, and everyone acknowledged the case would settle before trial, but I feared that, during my absence, one of the four other eager young associates on the team might uncover the proverbial smoking gun, and garner attention from the partners that would assure them an advantage in the well-paid rat-race we were engaged in. Besides, back then I was ambivalent about returning to the UK even for a brief visit, a ridiculous dread of somehow being dragged back into the swamp of my early childhood.

But I made it to the service after all. The parish church, built for a large congregation in the heyday of Victorian Anglicanism, was pleasingly crowded, and I thought I recognized some of my high school classmates crammed into the pews. I avoided their eyes as I seated myself. We had had nothing in common then, and I doubted that had changed. I could imagine having the same inane conversation, over and over.

"Wow, you look great! What are you up to? Wow, that's great! ….."

The priest, who looked too young for the job, was wrapping up his homily, a one-size-fits-all speech that made me think he had not known Miss Mumford well.

"And so, although we mourn the loss of a gentle soul, we are comforted by the conviction that she is at peace now. Is there anyone who would like to say a few words?"

I fleetingly thought perhaps I should go up to the front, but was happy to hear a shuffling a few rows behind that signaled someone else was taking up the invitation. A black man, a few years older than myself, a little portly in his Sunday suit, climbed the chancel steps.

"My name is Delroy Baines, and I work in the probation service in Portsmouth. I work with troubled youth.

"When I first went to live with Miss Mumford, *I* was the troubled youth. Fourteen years old, fresh out of the young offenders' center, and Miss Mumford was my last chance, if I didn't want to go back into custody for a really long stretch. I was mad as hell. Spitting mad. What could a little old white lady do for me?"

There was a little titter from the congregation. This was better than the priest's platitudes.

"I had a curfew. I was supposed to go straight to her place from school and stay there until it was time to leave for school the next morning. The very first time Miss M. had an evening meeting, I was out the door, on my way down to the pub on Wandsworth Common to hang out with the brothers. I was going to drink a few pints and then smoke dope on the Common. And if I didn't make it back to the house before she did, I didn't care.

"But things had changed while I'd been in detention. A new gang had taken over the pub. I thought, so what? I'll just ease in, impress them with my coolness and everything will be copacetic. "

Delroy shook his head and smiled out at the congregation.

"These blokes didn't think so. I had an elbow in my face within seconds and I was shown the door. I'm on the pavement outside trying to shake the bees out of my ears when I see that the

41

guy standing over me has a knife in his hand. They *really* didn't want me on their patch. That was OK. I'd've left, no problem, but the big guy wanted to make a point: this pub was *theirs*. So he got them all circled, me on all fours in the middle, their legs like tree trunks hemming me in. I knew they were going to kick the sh--, kick me to death, when I heard her voice. Miss Mumford, calling from the edge of the Common on the other side of the street, 'Have any of you young men seen my dog? He slipped his leash and ran over in this direction. Have you seen him? White terrier mix, just a small dog …'

"All the time she was talking, she was walking forward across the street. I wanted to yell at her to run. I was sure she was going to be knifed. But it was like a miracle. The gang just backed off. Six or seven real ugly goons just melted away, mumbling how they'd seen no dog, didn't want no trouble.

"She didn't say a word to me. I followed her home in a daze. She could have called the police as soon as she found me missing. That would have been the obvious, easy thing to do. I'd have gone back into detention, if I'd survived the beating outside the pub. But she didn't. Because of her courage, I'm here today."

I ducked my head down to hide the sudden moisture in my eyes. I glanced along the row: people were nodding to each other, sighing, and gripping tissues. I wished I had stayed in closer touch with Miss Mumford. At first, I had written regularly. After college, when she had made her one and only visit to the States to be the "family" at my graduation, our contact had gradually dwindled to Christmas cards. It was too late now to thank her for changing my life.

***

I glanced at my watch: two-thirty pm.   It was already night-time in London. The lights across the river from Dykstra's flat would be taking over the sky, turning it orange. In about thirty minutes, he would call. My determination to cut him off, made minutes before, was already weakening. I still didn't know whether to trust him. Was he as much a random victim of events as me, or was he somehow complicit in the chain that led from the Middle East to London and now to Atlanta. To answer that question, I must put aside the sexual attraction that undermined my objectivity.

Knowledge is power. Miss Mumford hadn't known Google from Gogol, but she was still pointing the way for me. I needed more information about Dykstra and I had thirty minutes and an Internet connection to get it. Scattering the last crumbs of chocolate heedlessly over the rug, I headed for my office and the computer.

He had been working on a story when he first met Lelana in Jordan in May. Before Amman, he had been working – on the same story? – in Egypt. I typed in "Pieter Dykstra," then "Europ News," the name of his press agency, and "Amman." I sifted through the first page of results, most of which led me back to his Europ News' website bio, then tried again, this time without Dykstra's name, and adding "Egypt" to "Amman." There were dozens of pages of results. Clearly, Europ News had been covering the Middle East for some time. The most recent hits were listed first. Half way down the second page, I found an article bylined Europ News that had been picked up by the Washington Post in June: "*Mid-East Rulers Hide Wealth Abroad.*" I scanned the first paragraph that laid out how dictators, including the King of Jordan, Mubarak in Egypt and Hassad in Syria, had salted away untold millions in Swiss bank accounts. I pressed the link to the rest of the article.

"However, under pressure from the U.S., banking regimes have become less accommodating to those who want to keep their wealth secret. Measures to prevent the funding of terrorists have forced even the closed-mouth Swiss to disclose account

43

information. Rulers seeking a safe depositary for the money obtained through corrupt practices are now looking to other solutions such as converting cash into diamonds which are compact, portable and relatively liquid."

I didn't need to read the rest of the piece to put together the puzzle, but I did anyway. It confirmed my conclusion. Against the day when they might fall from power, Middle East dictators were buying diamonds, often from illegal West African sources – "black diamonds" - to be stored with "friends" in Europe, or sold on the diamond markets in Antwerp or New York and the proceeds recycled into a variety of anonymous investments.

So, Lelana might be a courier. And the little bronze sphinx, purchased for $50 in a Cairo bazaar, might contain a king's ransom in diamonds. If Dykstra wrote the article, which he almost certainly did, he must have realized the sphinx's significance as soon as I told him it had been stolen. Unless he already knew what it contained. Unless *he* was the courier, or at least Lelana's partner in the smuggling plan. In which case, he had deliberately used me to transport the diamonds into the US, where an accomplice had broken into my house to pick them up. But if he was Lelana's partner in crime, why was she so put out when he gave me the sphinx in London? I was sure I had not imagined her reaction. And why had she come to my house to get the sphinx back, if I had just been a mule in the chain? Who was using who in this triangle?

I suppose I should have felt disappointed, even betrayed, by this new information, but strangely I was energized, like I had been doused in a cold shower. Now I had some facts to get my teeth into.

The phone rang.

"Sarah?"

I launched straight in.

"Lelana's here. Not here at the house, but in Atlanta. She *was* at the house—"

44

"I know. She used my credit card for her airline ticket. I feel awful—"

I cut him off. I had no time for this "poor me" stuff. Although I could not ignore the sexual current that pulsed through the phone line, I was on guard now.

"When were you going to tell me about the sphinx?"

The silence hung for a few seconds. I wasn't about to break it. I could sense Dykstra thinking it through and asking himself how much did I know.

"Look, I didn't want to involve you. I was on the trail of a story. I had my suspicions about Lelana, that she might be running diamonds, but I didn't know exactly how. It wasn't until you told me that the sphinx had been stolen that I put it together. By then, she had gone."

So all that making out in the restaurant and the concern he expressed for Lelana when he escorted me to the elevator was play-acting? He'd had me convinced. And if he was pretending so artfully then, what about now?

"And the gunman at the hotel?"

"I'm not sure. It could be someone sent by the man she jilted in Jordan – that story's true, she was escaping from an arranged marriage – or maybe she was planning to keep the diamonds for herself. Perhaps they found out and tried to punish her."

"Who's "they"?

"I don't know."

I drummed my fingers on the coffee table in exasperation. This was a tangled ball of string with a dozen loose ends. I hated loose ends.

"Look, I'm coming to Atlanta. That's where the trail leads." Dykstra changed to a more tentative voice, "Can I see you?"

I was too old for roller-coasters. Half an hour before, I had been determined to turn my back on Dykstra and the mystery of the sphinx; now, I was absorbed in working out the angles of an international intrigue. And still, in spite of my better judgment, I wanted to see the man again, although I suspected I could not trust him.

"O.K. but no more lies. I want to get to the bottom of this, but you have to be honest with me. "

He laughed, sounding suddenly boyish and excited.

"O.K! Partners, right?"

"Hmm. We'll see." I was smiling in spite of myself as I put the phone down.

Chapter 6

The weather changed in the night. The tail-end of a tropical storm that dumped two inches of rain on Florida was making its way north. Since I had returned from London five days ago, each morning had dawned crystal clear, and by afternoon the temperature was in the seventies, a gentle breeze shimmering the sunlit autumn leaves. But at four a.m. on Wednesday, I woke to the sound of rain rattling against the window, and an ominous creaking from the large oak tree that shaded the house. I comforted myself with the thought that the tree had withstood worse storms than this in its century of life. As an alternative to counting sheep, I tried to lull myself back to sleep by listing the things I would grab if I was forced to make a run for it. The laptop, certainly: it had all my work files and my address book. My Blackberry contained important phone numbers such as my insurance agent's, as well as my calendar. I would need my passport, my wallet with credit cards and drivers license – oh, and that cheat sheet of passwords which was tucked into my desk drawer. That should do it. A modern life that could be packed into a shoulder bag.

The cinema in my mind played images of haggard people picking over the debris in a trailer park the morning after a tornado. In voices choked with tears, they tell the TV news reporter how they're looking for childhood mementos, photograph albums, any remnant of the past. That would not be my problem. *My* problem was burying those childhood memories deep enough so that they would never be found. The tree's groans settled into a rhythm, and my thoughts drifted around untethered by any purpose or theme, until I floated away with them.

I was in a large public space – perhaps a shopping mall or an airline terminal, with people sauntering to and fro around me. I was irritated: the crowd's meanderings obscured my quarry, a figure in a long beige raincoat and old-fashioned Fedora pulled down hard over his head. He glided away from me, while my feet were mired in molasses. Now, it wasn't just people preventing me from keeping the figure in my line of sight; there were handcarts, little stalls selling brilliantly colored scarves and glittery gimcrack jewelry, encroaching on me from all sides, narrowing the path ahead. The stallholders grabbed at my sleeves, thrusting their faces into mine as they hawked their wares. The airline terminal had become an eastern bazaar; the noise, the heat and the smells conspiring to frustrate my pursuit. I glimpsed the figure turn aside into an alley. I pushed past the outstretched arms and made a strenuous effort to catch up. I made it to the mouth of the alley and felt a sudden spurt of elation: it was a cul-de-sac. But my elation changed to overwhelming dread as the figure in the raincoat slowly turned to face me.

"Dad!"

I shot upright in bed, staring wildly around the room. It took several seconds for my heart to resume its normal place in my chest and my gasps to quiet down to ordinary breathing. Ominous shapes settled back into the outlines of my bedroom furniture, gray in the half-light of dawn. The nightmare melted away like mist over water. I made no effort to recall it.

Wednesday. A week ago I had been in London, wrapping up a successful mediation and anticipating a solitary but celebratory dinner at the hotel before heading home to immerse myself in preparations for the next case. Now I was snarled in intrigue, attracted to a man I could not completely trust, and distracted from my work, the central thing that gave my life meaning and structure, not to mention how I earned my daily bread. I *must* get back into a routine. The night before, I had promised myself I would start the day with a three-mile run. Looking out the window at the pounding rain, I knew this would be impossible. Even if the rain let up, the going would be too treacherous for running. The storm had dislodged yesterday's fluttering gold leaves and they were now lying across the sidewalk in slimy brown drifts. But I needed a workout desperately. I debated whether my week-old wound was sufficiently healed to swim laps at the Y, and decided that, with a generous coat of Vaseline and an outsized waterproof Band-aid, I could risk it.

Although I now made enough money to join a ritzier health club, I stayed faithful to the Decatur YMCA. I liked its solid, family-friendly atmosphere and the variety of race, age and body types amongst the regulars. I didn't have to compete here with tanned twenty-somethings clad in designer fitness gear. I even liked the smell of the no-frills women's locker room: a mixture of chlorine and warm bodies. I quickly peeled off the sweats I had put on over my Speedo swimsuit, spent a few seconds under the shower, and headed for the pool.

Each lane was occupied, but as I stood there considering my options, a grizzled Leviathan arose sputtering at my feet, shedding water off his hairy shoulders.

"Ah'm jus' about finished, hon. Y'all kin share with me for a couple of laps, 'n then yer on yer own."

Before I could say thanks, he dove back under the water for another lap, causing a minor tsunami to engulf the neighboring swimmers. I waited a polite ten seconds, and then eased away from the side of the pool in his wake.

Within a couple of minutes, I was in the blissful, mindless zone of physical effort. I counted strokes and concentrated on my breathing, not noticing when my lap-swim companion climbed out of the pool, or what was happening in the neighboring lanes. I was surprised to see, when I raised my head out of the water at a turn, that I had been swimming for more than thirty minutes. I did a few cool-down laps, and then pulled myself out onto rubbery legs. A workout without sweating – what a concept. I resolved to make swimming a more frequent part of my fitness routine.

I was feeling so good about my healthy new start that I allowed myself a stop on the way home at the Dogwood Café. "The Dog" had been an institution in the neighborhood long before I moved in. Back then it had been a greasy spoon, a "breakfast served all day" kind of place. The food was good and filling, the proprietor, Saul, was welcoming, and I got in the habit of eating there with Gerardo after we finished some house project or other. About two years ago, Saul's daughter Heather returned home from Los Angeles where she had been trying to break into films, and she took over from the succession of behind-the- counter help Saul had employed to serve the customers while he did the cooking. There followed an uncomfortable period during which Heather attempted to force West Coast ideas into the traditional eatery over her father's vocal objections. Each would appeal for support to whatever customer had the misfortune to be sitting at the counter, quietly drinking their coffee and trying to enjoy their meal. Saul was small and wiry, and had all the excitability of his Sicilian ancestry. Heather, a head taller and striking-looking if not beautiful, had the benefit of drama school. Besides an undeniable presence, she had the ability to project her voice to every corner of the café.

I had more or less given up on the Dog, tired of the bickering, when a compromise was reached. Saul allowed the introduction of a new espresso machine – it was Italian-made, after all – and added some artisan breads and pastries to the menu. Heather put up a community notice board which displayed fliers for yoga lessons and the alternative bands that played at Decatur's edgier venues like the Trackside and Eddie's Attic. The booths, with their shiny red plastic seating, stayed, as did the ever-popular breakfast specials, although organic eggs were offered at an extra charge of fifty cents each.

The catalyst for the truce was the opening of a Starbucks down the block. This was a wake-up call to Saul who had previously scoffed at the idea that "his" customers would pay $3.50 for coffee. "His" customers proved only too willing to forego the Dog's cholesterol-heavy fare and its perfectly acceptable drip coffee to fork out for froth and previously-frozen bran muffins at Starbucks. Heather devised a clever publicity campaign to draw folks back to "Walkin' the Dog – your all-local, all-fresh neighborhood coffee shop and diner." Gradually, the defectors returned, and the customers who never left adjusted to the new touches. Father and daughter began to enjoy their partnership, and even to play up their contrasting styles for the entertainment (rather than the embarrassment) of the customers.

Heather was on duty behind the counter when I entered, my hair still damp from swimming, and nothing but the glow of exercise to enhance my complexion. Her hennaed locks were styled in a rakish geometric cut; a rose tattoo peeked shyly above the scoop neck of her mango-colored tee shirt. She was probably close to my age, but still affected the look and language of a teenager. I have to say it was working pretty well for her.

"Hiya, stranger! Whassup?"

"I've been traveling for work. How are you doing?"

"Oh, not too bad. I got Dad to make a morning glory muffin with pumpkin seeds and carrots – you gotta try it."

"OK, let me have one with a double-shot, non-fat latte – for here."

As Heather expertly wielded the knobs and levers that delivered the espresso shots, and sketched a pretty curlicue in the foam, I picked up the store copy of the *Atlanta Constitution* and climbed onto the closest seat at the counter.

"Did you see about that girl they found?"

I scanned the front page.

"What girl? I don't see anything in here."

"No, it was on the TV this morning. A body up by Agnes Scott." Heather was referring to the all-women liberal arts college across the railroad tracks. "She was shot, execution-style." Heather mimed a pistol with two fingers, pointed it at her temple, then rolled her eyes back in her head to demonstrate death. I felt like clapping.

"Was she a student?"

"Don't know. 'Unidentified body' is what they said. They had a sketch – I guess a photo would have been too gruesome – and were asking for anyone who knew her to get in touch." Heather shuddered. "So young …. It makes you think, doesn't it?"

"Hmm." Actually, I didn't want to think about it. The local TV news had a habit of over-dramatizing everything: a simple burglary became a "home invasion" and even the weather forecast was re-labeled a "Storm Watch." This probable suicide by a depressed young woman, sad though it was, was now elevated to a mob killing.

Heather moved off to serve another customer and I finished my muffin and coffee in peace. The rain had let up by the time I left the Dog. A strong wind was tearing apart the clouds and dispatching them to the north, leaving a clear blue sky behind it. It had turned much colder, though, and I hurried to my car, eager to get back to my cozy home office and to plunge into work before the feeling of well-being engendered by exercise and hot coffee could wear off.

After several productive hours on the computer, I was taking a break out back, stretching my back and shoulders and making mental lists of what needed to be done to prepare the yard for winter, when I heard my phone ring. I rushed back inside and picked up the Blackberry just as the caller abandoned hope and

52

disconnected. I checked the "missed call" list and recognized the number as Gerardo's. This was a surprise. He never called me, except to return *my* call. He was embarrassed about his English, and, without visual cues, he found phone conversations difficult. This must be important if he was initiating the call. I pressed his number immediately.

"Sarah? Is me, Gerardo. You see TV about the dead lady, the one at the college?"

"I heard about it, but I didn't see it on TV. Why? What's the matter?" Gerardo's voice, usually a warm rumble, had a higher pitch that indicated nervousness.

"She the one at the house. The one in the car with the man yesterday."

"No! Are you sure? I thought they just had a sketch." At first, I could not take in what Gerardo was saying. He must be mistaken. How could someone who had been in this very room yesterday now be dead?

"They have a picture now, and clothes she wear – same. I see it on TV jus' now. I'm sure it is same. I call you because I don' wan' …." Gerardo's voice trailed off in a sigh. I understood at once: he could not go to the police to identify her, putting himself and his family at risk of deportation. Anyway, he didn't know as much about her as I did. It was up to me to come forward, and to keep him out of it.

"It's alright, Gerardo. I'll look at the picture. If you're right, I'll go to the police. There's no need for you to worry. There's no reason why you should be involved."

"Thank you, Sarah. I don' wan' you be in trouble for this. Is dangerous, maybe? I can help. I stay on porch and guard you?" I smiled to myself at the picture of Gerardo performing sentry duty on the porch with his chain saw at the ready.

"No, I'm sure I'll be alright. I can't think of any reason why I'd be in danger." The moment the words were out of my mouth, I remembered the wound on my upper arm. It seemed to pulse with a sympathetic twinge of uneasiness, but perhaps that was just this morning's energetic swim. "I'll call you and tell you what happens. Don't worry."

After I hung up, I sat down on the sofa to take in Gerardo's call. Unlike the local TV station, Gerardo was *not* prone to exaggeration. If he thought the dead woman was Lelana, it was her. Who had killed her and why had she been killed? I found myself staring at the small rectangle in the center of the table where the sphinx had sat for its brief sojourn in my house. If - *when* - I went to the police, how much should I say? That Lelana was a diamond smuggler? That she had come to my house only hours before her death to retrieve a small statue that may have contained contraband, a statue that I had reported stolen the day before? That I had met her in London a week ago in the company of an investigative journalist who was on the trail of Middle East dictators' hidden assets? It all sounded improbable, as overdone as the lead story on the evening news. Given the cops' disinterest in the burglary on Monday, I could imagine their scarcely disguised sneers when I attempted to link it to the dead woman. I would be written off as a pre-menopausal hysteric.

But my first step was to satisfy myself that Gerardo was right and it *was* Lelana's body that had been found. I went to the laptop and opened a bookmarked link to AJC.com, the local daily's webpage. I was utterly unprepared to be confronted with Lelana's dead face, eyes closed, skin pale, but unmistakably her. I flinched and turned away from the screen, flashing back to the nightmare that had woken me that morning, experiencing the same horror and panic that made my heart flop around like a fish on the dock. I made myself look back at the screen.   The headline read, "*Woman's Body Found Near College.*" The photo underneath had obviously been retouched to clean up any signs of violence, the luxuriant black hair arranged carefully.   I had to read the accompanying text twice to take it in. She had been found about five a.m. next to dumpsters behind the college refectory by a kitchen helper arriving for the breakfast shift. The cause of death appeared to be a gunshot wound to the head. There was no identification on the body, which was dressed in jeans, a light-colored cotton jacket and black leather boots. A preliminary medical examination showed a female in her twenties, possibly of Southern European, Middle-Eastern or South American origin, height 5 foot 10 inches, weight 140 pounds. Anyone with information was urged to call the Decatur Police Department at ....

It was Lelana. There was no doubt. I thought about that first evening in the restaurant: how vivacious and exotic she had seemed as she tossed her hair away from her face. Then at Dykstra's apartment: the elegant way she had uncoiled herself from the white leather sofa when I arrived, and later, her slim brown hand trailing over the back of Dykstra's neck as she passed behind him to fetch more tea. Our final meeting yesterday: she had been jittery, her eyes flashing from side to side, but still beautiful, still full of life. I would not pretend to have liked her, but her death – the violent erasure of someone so young and lovely – was an offense against nature.

I reached for my phone and carefully entered the DPD's number.

Chapter 7

"Morgue" seemed an inappropriate name for the building I was directed to on the phone by the homicide detective handling the case. I imagined something dark and Victorian, not the glass and steel building in an office park next to I-85, but the Georgia Bureau of Investigation's crime lab was also housed there, requiring, I guessed, the modern, high-tech facilities.

I arrived after five-thirty, and the place was quiet, the parking spaces in front of the entrance mostly empty. There was no one sitting at the reception desk, but a tall thin black man dressed in jeans and a leather jacket was pacing the lobby. He approached with his hand outstretched.

"Sarah McKinney? I'm Detective John Dobey; we spoke on the phone."

After flashing me a microsecond look at his badge, he indicated that I should follow him to the back of the building and along a bland, windowless corridor. Some of the closed doors we passed bore names, others, familiar-sounding acronyms: "CSI Support," "DEA Liaison." There was no way of knowing whether live bodies toiled behind the doors. We saw no one and, except for our footsteps on the vinyl floor, there was silence. I felt a twinge of nervousness. The place was too quiet. No one knew I was here. Dobey opened an unlabeled door and led me into an anonymous-looking room furnished with a plain table and four molded plastic chairs – an interview room, not anyone's office. It felt Kafka-esque. Dobey sensed my unease and smiled reassuringly, as he indicated a chair. I sat down across from him, looking around for a two-way mirror. There was none, but up in the corner of the ceiling a small camera was pointed at my seat, a pinprick of red light flashing on and off every two seconds.

"Is that thing on?" I indicated the camera with an inclination of my head.

"Oh, no," the detective replied with a chuckle. "The red light means it's on stand-by. I make a record the old fashioned way." He lifted up a notebook in one hand and a pen in the other. I didn't know if I believed him, but there was little I could do about it. Dobey opened his notebook and got down to business.

"I really appreciate you coming in after hours. If we wait to identify the body until tomorrow, the traces might be cold. Every minute counts in a murder investigation."

"You're sure it's murder then? Not suicide or some weird accident?"

"Yeah, we're pretty sure. Now tell me again who you think this woman is, and how you met her." He kept eye contact, looking at me expectantly, pen poised over the notebook page.

"I only know her first name: Lelana. I met her for the first time in London last week, and then she came to my house yesterday. She's Jordanian, or perhaps Lebanese. I think she was studying in London. I believe she flew in from London on Monday evening. I suppose they'll have some customs and immigration records at the airport."

Dobey looked up from his notes, waiting for me to say something else, but I had seen clever lawyers use this trick in depositions, and had used it myself on occasions: usually the interviewee, uncomfortable with the silence, breaks it to volunteer more information. Often the most important evidence is discovered this way. I remained quiet. After a few seconds, the detective smiled and gave a little sigh, conceding defeat.

"OK, so why did this Lelana come to see you in Atlanta? Did you know she was coming here?"

"No, I was surprised to see her." I was on the point of telling him that she came to reclaim the sphinx, but stopped myself. Stubbornness, I guess, but I wanted to make him work for it.

Dobey tried the silence tactic again. He seemed to be enjoying the game.

"And?" He said finally. I looked at him questioningly. "Why did she come to see you?"

"She was looking for a little statue I had been given in London last week. A bronze sphinx. She said it belonged to her. But I didn't have it. It was taken in a break-in at my home on Monday. There should be a report with your department. She seemed upset I didn't have it any longer. She didn't stay long," I finished lamely.

"Did she say where she was staying? What her plans were?"

I was relieved to get away from the reason for her visit to me, and onto safer ground where I felt comfortable responding.

"No. There was someone waiting for her in the car. A man."

"Did you get a look at him? Did she say who he was?"

"No, she didn't mention him. I just saw him when she left. He'd gotten out of the car. Tall, well-built, shaved head. Maybe Middle-Eastern ....?" I let my voice trail off uncertainly. I certainly didn't want to get into Gerardo's role with the chain saw.

"Middle-Eastern? Like her?" He pounced on the lead. I realized I had probably said enough, and just shrugged, retreating into vagueness.

After another long pause during which Dobey looked at me appraisingly, he flipped the notebook closed.

"Hmm. Well, let's go see if this woman is your Lelana." Dobey pushed back his chair and stood, indicating I should precede him out into the corridor. We went back to the still-empty lobby, where he pressed the elevator button, and we descended to the basement. It was cooler down there, and there was a slight chemical odor that brought back a sensory memory of the YMCA pool that morning. I followed him along a dimly lit corridor. The detective punched in a code to open a door at the end. Inside, a white-coated attendant in rubber boots was washing down an examination table with a hose.

"Hey, Leon. Can you show us the body that was brought in this morning? The woman?"

"Sure, just wait here."

"Leon" disappeared behind a partition. Dobey still had his notebook in his hand and he was tapping it rhythmically with his pen while we waited. I concentrated on taking slow deep breaths, trying to calm the flutter in my chest that I knew from experience presaged a panic attack. The realization that I was about to be confronted with a dead body undermined my usual self-control.

Leon returned, wheeling a gurney. The body on it was covered with a white sheet. Dobey gently put a hand under my elbow.

"Are you ready?" he asked.

I swallowed and nodded. Leon folded back the sheet to reveal just the head and shoulders of the dead woman. One glance was enough to confirm it was indeed Lelana. The hair – still lustrous and thick – was unmistakable. Her skin looked pale with a bluish tone. The lips still bore traces of the Chinese red lipstick she favored.

"Yes, it's her." I turned away and took a deep breath. "Can we go now?" I walked quickly back to the door. I had to get out of this room and back up to the fresh air. Dobey loped along beside me. Back in the lobby, he held my arm.

"Are you OK? Do you want to sit down for a minute?"

"No, I just want to get out of here. I've … I've never seen a dead body before. She was … Yesterday, she was at my house, and now … " I knew I was rambling, that I should just shut up and focus on breathing in and out, putting one foot in front of the other until I could escape this place, but I felt disoriented. My legs were weak, and I was grateful for Dobey's supporting grip.

"Is there anything else you can think of? Any reason why she would be killed?"

I looked at him, his question reverberating around my brain. He was, after all, a smart interrogator: wait for a moment of weakness, then pry the key information loose. This was the moment to tell him about Dykstra's investigation, his theory that Lelana was a mule carrying diamonds or other contraband for corrupt Middle-Eastern rulers; that the little sphinx he had given me might be a hiding place. I could describe Lelana's panic when she found out I no longer had the sphinx. Was her death the punishment for failing to recover the statue? It sounded lurid and far-fetched, hysterical even. I flashed back again to the two Decatur police officers smirking at my assumption that they would dust my house for fingerprints after the break-in, their casual dismissal of the possibility that the burglar would be caught. Even if Dobey took my story seriously, would he have the resources he'd need to follow it up? No, he would do his best to identify Lelana's killer from the leads I'd given him, before the next drive-by shooting or abusive husband's drunken attack claimed his attention.

"No, I can't think of anything else." I held his gaze, feeling calmer now, my routine defenses back in place. We moved together towards the glass doors to the parking lot.

"Well, if anything else occurs to you, you have my number. Thanks for your help. I'll follow up with Customs and

Immigration, the car rental agencies at the airport, and the hotels. We should be able to get a complete ID pretty soon."

We parted ways outside. He headed to a fast-looking, low-slung car, black, maybe a Camaro. I climbed into my ten-year-old Accord; I've never been much of a car person. I dug into my purse to retrieve my Blackberry before I started the engine. I had silenced the phone before I went into the building, and I wanted to check for messages. There were two missed calls, both from the same number, but no voicemails. No new emails either. The number had enough digits to signal that it was an international call. Dykstra? But it was the middle of the night in London.

As I pulled away from the building, I began to second guess my reticence with Detective Dobey. I was so accustomed to using the possession of information to assert authority in my work life – Miss Mumford's mantra, "knowledge is power" had become my own – that I had naturally resisted Dobey's attempts to dig deeper into my acquaintance with Lelana. Another pressure to keep silent was my fear of appearing over-dramatic and provoking the "there, there, little woman" reaction I so detested. In this case, had these impulses overcome good sense? After all, the man seemed smart, and even if he wasn't, it was my duty to tell him everything I knew or thought I knew. I reluctantly acknowledged another reason I hadn't said anything about the diamond smuggling: to do so would reveal Dykstra's role. For some motive that I wasn't proud of, I wanted to keep Dykstra to myself. Last time we had spoken, he had suggested that we could be partners on the trail of the little sphinx. Like a fourteen-year-old at the school dance, I was saving myself for him, spurning other partners while I waited for the lights to dim and the slow music to start. What an idiot!

I stopped off at Whole Foods for something for dinner. I hadn't eaten since the muffin at the Dog that morning, and in spite of the unsettling visit to the dead woman at the morgue (or perhaps because of it?) I was starving. I selected a Thai curry dish with rice and some salad rolls, and picked up a bottle of Prosecco to go with the meal. I justified the bubbly by telling myself that, in the near presence of death, I was celebrating life. Anyway, my usual red wine would taste like vinegar with all that spice. While I was at the store, I browsed the shelves for other staples I needed, so it was getting dark by the time I emerged to drive the last couple of miles home.

Traffic was light on the tree-lined streets. In many of the little ramblers and larger mock colonials, lights had been turned on, but drapes left open, allowing me to spy on glowing vignettes of life in the suburbs. Halloween was still a few weeks off, but some eager families had already decorated their porches with pumpkins; a few had gone the whole hog with ghosts and witches in the trees, and fake gravestones on immaculate front lawns. I made a mental note to lay in some candy. In other years, I had dressed as a witch in flowing black, put on green make-up and a store-bought pointy hat, but I doubted whether I'd be in the mood this year.

I was slowing down to turn into my driveway when a dark shape at the top of my porch steps caught my eye. It was boxy with rounded ends, a duffel bag, perhaps. At the same instant I caught a movement further back on the porch. Another intruder? I rapidly considered what to do: call the police? Yeah, and wait twenty minutes for them to come and make fun of me. Call Gerardo? He'd come, but it would take him twenty minutes too, and it wasn't fair to disturb his family time. Go to a neighbor's house? That seemed the best option. I aborted my turn into the driveway and slowed to a crawl, easing the car past the house as I craned sideways over the passenger seat to get a clearer look at the front porch. I was just deciding which of my pleasant but not overly-close neighbors to grace with my presence when a male figure appeared at the top of my porch steps. He waved hesitantly, as if not sure who I was. It was Dykstra.

I pulled the car to the curb and turned off the engine. Feeling dazed, I got out and walked back towards the house. Dystra was rushing down the steps and along the path. We met in the driveway, standing face to face, six feet apart. He gave me the wide boyish grin I remembered from that first time in the hotel restaurant, and I felt a familiar melting feeling starting in my stomach and spreading lower down.

"Hi, this is ... a surprise. What are you doing in Atlanta?" I struggled to speak evenly.

"I told you yesterday on the phone. Don't you remember? I'm following Lelana, trying to get to the bottom of the smuggling story I started in the Spring."

My stomach gave another lurch; this time it was more like a locomotive hitting my solar plexus. Dykstra didn't know about Lelana's murder.

Chapter 8

After I let Dykstra and his black duffel bag into the house, I bought myself some time by retrieving the car from the curb where I had abandoned it. As I maneuvered the Honda into the garage at the back of the lot, I worried about how to tell him that Lelana had been murdered. After all, they had been lovers, even though she had recently left him, and even though he had perhaps been using her to track down a story. I kept thinking of their faces that night in the hotel restaurant: they had been so happy! Whatever other motives muddied their affair, there was no denying, at least that evening, they shared the kind of glow that arouses envy even in the contentedly single like myself. How would he react to learning of her death?

I checked my face and hair in the rear view mirror before I unloaded the groceries and headed for the back door. I was glad I had changed into narrow-cut black pants and a blue-gray cashmere cowl-neck sweater before my visit to the morgue. Of course, I could never compete with Lelana's vibrant beauty, but I was confident in my own more restrained style. Then I remembered Lelana's pallid face at the morgue, and choked on my remorse. I was ashamed of indulging in a "who's the prettiest" contest with a murdered woman.

Chastened, I fumbled two bags of groceries onto one arm, and unlocked the back door with my other hand. After I put the bags down on the counter, I stood for a moment looking through the arch that separated the kitchen from the living room. Dykstra was standing in the center of the room, looking around appreciatively at my furniture and art work: the Stickley armchair for which I had saved for years, the bird's eye maple dining table, salvaged and painstakingly restored. It struck me that he was standing in exactly the same spot that Lelana had occupied the previous day. Before he could complete the weird parallel by coming out with the same compliment about my beautiful house, I blurted the bald facts, making no attempt to soften them.

"Lelana's dead. Her body was found early this morning on a college campus near here. She was shot through the head."

I felt like an idiot. I was supposed to be a skilled communicator, able to predict and steer the extremes of emotions that high stakes mediations often generate. Instead, I had panicked. What was it about this man that robbed me of my self- possession, my cool professional persona?

For a couple of seconds, Dykstra looked at me with his expression unchanged, a politely interested gaze, as if it took time for the shocking news to travel across the dozen feet that separated us. Then his face seemed to melt and drain of color, the mouth sagging open, the eyes squeezed shut. He even staggered forward a little. He made no sound.

"I'm so sorry," my voice was now a hoarse whisper. "I didn't know how to break it to you. I've just come from identifying the body. She didn't have any ID on her. They put her picture on the TV and the web, looking for witnesses. I recognized her photo. It's hard to believe – she was here, just yesterday."

As I spoke, I crossed to him and guided him to a seat on the sofa, keeping a hand on his arm to steady him. He dragged his other hand over his face, breathing deeply, before he visibly pulled himself together and turned toward me.

"Are you sure it's her?"

"Yes." I was familiar with the stages of grief; denial was often the first reaction. But Dykstra merely nodded slowly.

"Tell me again, how—how did she die?"

"She was shot in the back of the head. Her body was found about five a.m. this morning by someone on his way to work at the college. I don't know if she died there or somewhere else, or exactly when she died. The police aren't giving too much away, but they're definitely treating it as murder. Do you think it was because of the sphinx? She seemed so upset yesterday that I didn't have it, and the man with her—"

"Did you tell the police about the man?" Dykstra asked urgently, "Or the sphinx?"

I was instantly on the alert. He seemed to have shrugged off his grief for Lelana, and was refocusing on his quest for a story. I replied hesitantly.

"Yes, I told the detective that she was looking for the sphinx but it had been stolen. He didn't ask any other questions about it. I don't know if he thought it was relevant. And I mentioned the man Lelana was with. The detective took down a description, and he thought that might be a lead. Anyway, he said they would try to trace her movements from her arrival at the airport up to her death, look at rental car records, and things like that. Do *you* think that man killed her because she couldn't retrieve the sphinx?"

"I don't know. It's possible." Like quicksilver, his mood had changed again. He slumped against the back of the sofa, staring vacantly ahead. He looked exhausted, and I remembered that for him it was the middle of the night.

"Look, let me get you a drink and something to eat. Then we can talk about it."

I escaped to the kitchen to put away the groceries and organize my thoughts. As I criss-crossed to the cupboards and the pantry, I glanced through to the sitting room. Dykstra remained seated on the sofa, eyes now closed.

Questions leapt at me from all sides. Who stole the sphinx from me, and how did they know I had it? Who was the man with Lelana yesterday, and did he kill her? But these were almost superficial questions. The real question I had to answer was, what was I doing getting involved? This had nothing to do with me and my well-ordered life. I should throw Dykstra out on his ear, double-lock the doors, take an Ambien and forget any of this had happened.

But, ridiculous as it sounded, I was attracted to the man now sprawled on my sofa. I almost laughed out loud. I thought of the corporate bigwigs and their expensive attorneys who sought out my services to resolve complex business disputes involving millions of dollars and thousands of employees. What would they think if they knew that someone with my reputation for professional neutrality and coolness under pressure was so seduced by an adolescent crush that she couldn't disentangle herself from a downward spiral of violence and intrigue? I thought of women I knew, decent, well-educated and attractive women, who , time after time, fell for men who were complete disasters: momma's boys who could not commit to a pizza topping, much less a relationship, or bullies who ignored and two-timed them. I had felt a superior kind of pity for these women, convinced I would never be so stupid. This was no different.

With a sigh, I contemplated the Thai curry, determining how to stretch it with rice noodles and frozen peas into a meal for two. I loaded a tray with plates, forks and glasses; chose a bottle of pinot gris (the Prosecco I had bought earlier now seemed entirely too celebratory for the occasion) and quickly defrosted some edamame. I boiled water for the noodles and peas and set the curry container in the microwave. Two minutes: time to heat the meal and decide a course of action. End it now, or plunge head first into

67

something that might be as dangerous to my life as to my peace of mind.

I carried the tray into the living room. Dykstra opened his eyes, and looked unsmiling straight into mine.

"Will you help me find Lelana's killers?"

I had made my decision before the microwave bell rang "time's up."

"Yes."

**

The meal revived him. We didn't speak of Lelana. He asked me questions about Atlanta and we talked about New York which he knew well, and where I had worked – I would never call it "lived" – for a few years after law school. I recognized again the charming and intelligent host who had so impressed me that evening in his London apartment. Yet lurking underneath, like a shark cruising the shallows where the tourists laughed and splashed, was the fact that a woman had been murdered.

There was another shark cruising the room too. It was close to ten p.m. Where was Dykstra planning to spend the night? He had not mentioned a hotel. Was he waiting for an invitation? We lapsed into silence as I poured the last of the wine into our glasses. I raised my head to find him looking at me with a quizzical look and the beginnings of a smile. He's reading my mind, I thought, and immediately blushed. Cursing the Scots-Irish ancestry that gave me such a vulnerable complexion, I buried my nose in my glass. What the hell, someone has to say something.

"Do you have a hotel room booked?"

"No," Looking at his watch. "I suppose I'd better call a cab."

"Well, you're welcome to stay here – on the sofa, I mean. I don't have a guest room, the second bedroom's my study, but the sofa's full-length ; it should be comfortable." Shut up! You're

68

babbling like a child! I bent my head again and began to pile the plates on the tray, just to occupy my hands. He reached out and held my wrist lightly, stopping my movement. A charge ran through me.

"Are you sure?" His voice was low and husky. Suggestive? Or just plain exhausted? I dragged my eyes up to his and nodded slowly. He continued to hold my wrist. At that moment, I wanted more than anything to kiss him. Something held me back. The thought that his girlfriend had just been murdered? Or, more likely, my perpetual fear of humiliation, of misreading the signs, and a premonition of Dykstra's aghast look if I lunged towards him. The moment passed.

"Thank you, Sarah." He slid his hand over the back of mine as he withdrew it. I picked up the tray and headed for the kitchen. With my back safely turned, I trusted myself to speak again.

"The bathroom's the door on the left. I'll get a pillow and blankets."

I put the tray down, and stood for a moment listening to my heart beat. I heard the bathroom door close, then stacked the dirty dishes in the dishwasher. After a few minutes, I went through to my bedroom where the extra duvet was stored. I put a fresh cover on one of my pillows and grabbed a couple of towels. I took a few steadying breaths, and walked back into the sitting room.

Dykstra was lying on the sofa, his hands across his stomach, eyes closed, chest rising and falling rhythmically. As I draped the duvet over him, he made a small satisfied sound – hmmmm – and settled deeper into sleep.

....

I'm an early riser, but Dykstra was awake and up before me. I woke a little before seven to the smell of coffee. I showered in a hurry, and pulled on jeans and a long-sleeved t-shirt. The sexual tension I had felt the evening before had dissipated in the

69

bright light of day. I was energized, ready for adventure, and primed with questions for Dykstra.

"Good morning. I hope you don't mind me helping myself." He indicated the coffee pot, and the toasted bagel on his plate.

"Of course not. Did you sleep well?"

"Not bad, and you?" I searched his face for any innuendo. There was none. He too was all business this morning.

"Yes, thanks." I replied, pouring myself some coffee and putting another bagel in the toaster. "So, what's the plan? Are you going to speak to the detective in charge of Lelana's case?"

"I don't think so, not yet. I want to go through all Lelana's movements since she left my flat on Monday afternoon. Then maybe you could show me where her body was found?"

"Mmm, I could, yes, but first, Pieter, I need you to fill me in. You haven't told me exactly what Lelana was mixed up in, or ….." I swallowed, "about your relationship with her. Was she really being forced into a marriage against her will? Were you using her as a source to get closer to the bad guys? If we are going to work together, you have to be completely honest—"

"O.K., O.K.!" He laughed a little nervously. "I'll tell you everything I know. It's probably a lot less than you think. And I'll tell you what I suspect. That's where I need your help; you can be my reality check. Sometimes you live with a story for so long, you lose touch with what's fact and what's speculation. Now, Lelana …." His voice trailed off, and I saw the pain of her loss again on his face.

"I met Lelana in Amman through a source, a woman I had been working with on the story I broke in May about Middle-Eastern dictators and their hidden assets. Lelana moved with a crowd of rich young people, the children of wealthy, highly placed men. These kids are well-educated – mostly in the UK or the US – and have nothing to do but travel and spend their family money.

Consequently, they get bored, and, as the saying goes, the devil finds work for idle hands. One of Lelana's ex-boyfriends   was caught in Turkey smuggling drugs, just for the thrill of it."

He paused to sip his coffee, then plunged on with the story.

" So, some of the older generation, government officials, those close to power, decided to enlist these young jet-setters to get their assets out of the country and invested in more stable currencies. At first, it was just a matter of depositing cash in phony accounts or shell corporations in Europe and the States, but lately the international financial authorities have been cracking down, so they had to turn to more creative solutions, such as "black" diamonds from Sierra Leone. They could smuggle them into Antwerp or New York and sell them to friendly gem merchants, then launder the proceeds by buying legitimate or semi-legitimate businesses. The problem is that dealing in illicit diamonds put these spoiled babies in touch with some very dangerous types. Of course, that was part of the attraction for some of them: playing in the underworld, taking risks with more than just money."

Dykstra told the story succinctly and impersonally, a skilled reporter setting out the facts.

"And Lelana's involvement ....?"

His voice softened. "My source said she wasn't involved in the smuggling, but knew the people who were. She told me that Lelana needed help – she really was being forced into an arranged marriage – and she might give me some leads in exchange for helping her to escape. That was our arrangement .... to start with. She introduced me to a couple of guys in her crowd, one was the son of an Egyptian government minister, the other was Lebanese. I've been out drinking with them a couple of times. I'm really close now to getting them to reveal more."

He looked away before continuing.

71

"I brought Lelana to London and hid her in my flat. I guess it seemed inevitable that we'd end up sleeping together. It's a very small flat." He glanced sheepishly back at me. "Stupid to think the attraction was mutual. She is—was – young and beautiful, and I'm …. Anyway, that evening in the hotel restaurant, I'd just got a call from Arun, the Egyptian, inviting us to go sailing with him in the Caribbean; he was going to fly us from London in his father's jet …. We were celebrating. It seemed like a breakthrough."

I saw him again in my mind's eye, kissing Lelana's painted lips, his hands buried in her jet black hair. I felt a sharp pang of sympathy for him. Of course, he had fallen for her. What man in his forties could resist such beauty, such youth? And he would never know now whether she was just using him, a plane ticket, a meal ticket, a place to hide until she could sort out something – someone – better. I sensed he was remembering the same image of Lelana in the restaurant, and I wanted to distract him.

"The man with the gun? Was he something to do with the smuggling?"

His tone became more matter of fact. "No, I don't think so. Lelana's aunt is a crazy Muslim fundamentalist. She was the one pressing for Lelana to be married off. I think when she found out that Lelana was living with an infidel in London, she decided her death would be better than the disgrace. Then you got in the way."

He smiled at me over his coffee cup. My stomach did a little jump, but I smiled back.

"So, where do we go from here?"

"Can I use this?" Dykstra indicated a small note pad I kept on the counter for making shopping lists.

"I'll get you something bigger." I quickly got a legal pad from my office and watched as he pulled off two sheets. He extracted a pen from his pocket and wrote "Lelana" in the center of one, and "sphinx" on the other. I liked his handwriting. He wrote fast, in competent, square upper case letters, and finished by drawing a box round each word.

"The question is: who knew Lelana was in Atlanta? Who did she tell or who was tracking her? Same question about the sphinx. Who knew it was here?" He looked up at me, inviting me to take a stab at an answer.

"Well, as far as Lelana's concerned, couldn't her aunt or her hired gun have followed her here? You said you didn't think the British police would hold them for long. And they've already shown they're ready to kill."

"Yes, that's possible." He drew a line from the "Lelana" box to the top left hand corner of the page and wrote "Aunt" and "Gunman." "That would mean her death is unrelated to the theft of the sphinx. Mmm. OK, let's assume that for the moment." He pulled the other page towards him, and stared at it, tapping the pen against his lips.

"If you're right and Lelana knew there was something hidden in the sphinx, who would she call when she knew you'd be bringing it to Atlanta last Friday? My pals Arun, the Egyptian, or Paul, the Lebanese guy, or one of their other friends. But could any of them organize a robbery on another continent over the weekend? They're amateurs."

"You said they had criminal connections."

Dykstra wrote "Arun" and "Paul" at the top of the sphinx page and connected the names to the center box. Then he drew another line ending in a query, the unknown criminal connection.

"To pull off the robbery on Monday morning, the criminal connection probably had to already have an established presence in Atlanta, or at least in the US. But if they had stolen back the sphinx, why did they need to kill Lelana?"

"So you *don't* think it was an honor killing, the crazy aunt?"

He sighed. "No, I don't. I think it's the rest of it – the sphinx, her murder, the asset smuggling, all of that. And I think the answer's here, in the U.S., but I don't know why ...."

Something Dykstra had told me earlier clicked into place. He might be the investigative journalist, but I had a well-tuned ear for tiny nuggets of information that could turn a case.

"Do you have Arun's number? I think you should call him and break the news about Lelana's death. His reaction might be instructive. And you could also find out when he's coming here on his way to that Caribbean sailing vacation."

A slow smile spread over Dykstra's face, the first real smile I had seen since I broke the news of Lelana's death. It stripped fifteen years off him, and turned my insides to jelly.

Chapter 9

I have a half-brother. His name was Shane. I suppose he's still out there somewhere. He left when I was five or six. I remember a lanky boy with pimples and a mop of wiry black hair falling over one side of his face. His eyes were huge and dark, and his dark cheeks had a permanently sucked-in look. Perhaps his eyes seemed big because he was so skinny. He must have inherited his looks from his unknown father; he had nothing of our mother's coloring: her dishwater fair hair, pale blue eyes, and small features.

I was furious with him when he ran away. I felt betrayed and abandoned. We had spent a lot of time together, probably because he got stuck with looking after me while my parents partied, and I relied on him as a kind of buffer against the so-called adults with their unpredictable swings between affection and violence. I can still hear Shane's voice, breathy and cracking in places as he sang me to sleep in the makeshift bed we shared: "Lola," "Jumpin' Jack Flash," "Hit The Road, Jack." Inappropriate lullabies, perhaps, but they echoed the soundtrack of our lives at that point: summers spent trailing from one rock festival to another, Reading to the Isle of Wight to Glastonbury, camping in a barn or half-ruined cottage. In the winter, we would retreat to London, where my father and his friends would "liberate from the bourgeoisie" some boarded-up tenement: "our socialist workers' commune," as Dad grandiosely named the rag-taggle group of tie-died potheads we lived with.

"Squatter's rights!" He'd scream, when the police finally reacted to the neighbors' complaints of loud music at all hours, smoke from cooking over open fires, and the stench of blocked-up drains. And then, "Fascist pigs!" This would guarantee a non-too gentle eviction and a couple of nights in a charity hostel until another likely squat was found.

My father had somehow wangled a student visa and come to England in 1968 to escape the Vietnam draft. He soon dropped out of whatever studies he was supposed to be pursuing, and drifted onto the fringes of the London rock scene. That was where he met my mother, already a seasoned groupie. The fact that she was also the mother of a four-year old child probably escaped him at first. After all, she was content to leave the boy with whatever long-suffering friend would keep him while she nudged herself closer to the rock star *du jour* – the one buying the booze or passing the weed.

I can't blame Shane for running away. Indeed, he became my role model when, about seven years later, I hit the road too. Even as a very young child, I think I understood the hell my father put him through. The event that pushed Shane out was when Dad found him noodling a tune on Dad's guitar.

"Put the goddamn guitar down, and get over here!" My father was enraged: *he* was the musician in the family, all on the strength of six months as a roadie for some third-rate band that thought they could fill the void when the Beatles broke up. He also claimed to have dropped acid with Jimi Hendrix in the back room at Ronnie Scott's, but that was later, when drugs had finally erased the line between reality and make-believe. I'm sure Dad's resentment against Shane had been building steadily since my mother moved in with him, bringing the dark little stranger with her. His fury was heightened on this occasion by the realization that Shane had a natural talent, while all Dad had ever been able to coax out of the instrument were three basic chords.

Although my father liked to present himself as a vagabond philosopher, a world traveler with socialist ideals, it didn't take much to reveal his small-minded, white-trash Southern roots, especially when he was on the downside of a high. As soon as Shane had put a little distance between himself and the precious Stratocaster, he grabbed a handful of the boy's T-shirt, and punched him hard on the side of the head with his other fist.

"You fucking nigger! You little coon-faced ass-wipe! Don't you ever, ever fucking touch my stuff again with your dirty little nigger paws!"

Shane could not fall down, although the first of the rain of blows was sufficient to lay him out. The older, bigger man's grip kept Shane upright, his head bouncing back like a punching bag at each blow, Dad's spittle glazing his cheeks, and blood trickling from his nose into his open mouth. Still the boy made no sound. It was only when I let out a strangled cry from my hiding place behind the sofa that Dad, still holding Shane up by his shirt, paused and looked around the room, as if surprised to find himself there. He let Shane drop and walked out without another word.

Later that day, Shane left.

***

I was sitting in my office struggling to concentrate on responding to emails, when my half-brother's image came to mind. Dykstra was in the living room making calls on his cell phone. From the low rumble of his voice, I picked out the word "Lelana," and thought of Shane. It must have been their similarity of coloring, the black hair and *café au lait* skin. Or perhaps the fear that his life had also ended violently, an anonymous victim lying under a sheet on a stainless steel shelf. Over the years, I had thought of him, hoping he had been able to separate himself from those sordid beginnings. I somehow doubted that he could have got as far away as I had. After all, he didn't have the advantage of my father's sole legacy to me: an American passport.

Usually, I'm all business once I enter my office. It was the smaller of the two bedrooms and I had cleared it of all distractions. One window faced the driveway and the blank wall of the neighbor's house; the other looked out at the trunk of the ancient water oak in the back yard. I had furnished the rest of the house in keeping with the Craftsman style, original pieces or modern reproductions, but here IKEA ruled. Clean lines, light wood and steel, lots of storage. The centerpiece was my computer standing sleekly in the center of my paperless desk. I moved the cursor up and down the screen, highlighting one e-mail subject line after another, but unable to make the simple decision to click one open. My thoughts wandered from Shane to Lelana to the previous evening, and I relived for a delicious moment Dykstra's hand lingering on mine. On cue, I looked up to find Dykstra leaning against the door frame, looking pleased with himself. If he noticed my sudden flush, he had the grace to pretend he didn't.

"How would you like to spend five fun-filled days, all expenses paid, cruising the blue seas of the Bahamas?" He asked , affecting a not very convincing American accent.

"What are you talking about?"

"I got through to Arun. He's in Paris. I told him about Lelana's murder. He seemed genuinely upset, but then it's hard to tell on the phone." He paused, looking away, and I wondered for the umpteenth time how genuine his own distress about Lelana was. "I managed to remind him about his invitation to go sailing. The trip's still on. He and Paul are flying to Atlanta at the weekend, then on to the coast where the yacht is berthed. There's a guy from New York, a banker or stock trader, I think. He's joining them with his girlfriend. Arun still wants me to come, and, I'm quoting here, they're 'short on babes' so I'm encouraged to bring a guest. Whaddya say?" He reverted to the phony accent.

I laughed. "I don't think I'm babe material."

He was beginning to protest when my cell phone rang. I picked it up off the desk and looked at the screen.

"It's the Decatur PD. Probably the detective I met yesterday, the investigator on Lelana's case."

"Great. Perhaps he has some new information."

"Well, I doubt he's calling to share it with me." I was uneasy about speaking to Dobey; I had not been completely forthcoming with him the day before, and I sensed that he knew it, but I accepted the call anyway. "Hello?"

"Hi. Ms. McKinney? This is Detective Dobey, calling about the Lelana Sherat case?"

I registered that this was the first time I had heard Lelana's last name.

"Yes, hi. So you've been able to confirm her identity?" Dykstra was leaning forward to hear both sides of the conversation. I was trying to think of other questions that would draw the detective out, but Dykstra's nearness was unsettling.

"Er, yes. Ms. Sherat entered the US on a Jordanian passport, and we notified their embassy. That's what I wanted to talk to you about."

The detective paused. He was the one who sounded nervous now. Dykstra and I exchanged puzzled looks.

"Look, this guy, the Jordanian Consul General, he called this morning and wants your name and contact information. He says that the next-of-kin may want to speak to you, seeing as how you may have been one of the last people to see her alive, but I didn't want to hand out the information without your say-so. Is it okay for me to do that, give him your information, I mean?"

Dykstra was frowning exaggeratedly, making a face I could not interpret. My first inclination was to refuse, and protect my privacy at all costs, but I realized that an opportunity to speak to Lelana's family might offer some clues as to the identity of her killer. I stalled for time.

"I .... I don't know. Let me think about it. Can I call you back?"

Dobey sighed.

"Yeah, I guess so. Can you get back to me today? You have my number?"

"I do. And thanks, I mean, for not just giving them my name. I appreciate it."

"Sure. Look, if you have any other information, I need you to give it to me. Don't hold back on me."

I looked at Dykstra for a lead. He shrugged, and leaned back, leaving me to make my own decision.

"Well, it's just a hunch. Lelana was really upset that I no longer had the statue, and the big man with her looked pretty angry about it too. Have you found out who he was? Maybe ... " I trailed off.

"Maybe he was angry enough to kill her? Yeah, we thought of that."

After I disconnected, we sat with our separate thoughts for a minute. Then Dykstra broke the silence.

"There's no way of knowing if it really was the Jordanian Consul that called the local police."

A little tingle of fear ran through me, but I shook it off, and stood up abruptly.

"You said you wanted to see where Lelana's body was found. I'm getting nothing done here." I gestured at the computer screen. "Let's walk over to the college. We can discuss it on the way."

"Alright, and we can talk about the Bahamas too. I bet you look great in a bikini."

***

Yesterday's rain had signaled a change of seasons. Indian summer was over, and although the sky was clear, the sun was weak and a chill mist blurred the outlines of the trees and houses. I hunched down inside my thick sweater as I strode alongside Dykstra. I liked the way he accommodated his pace to mine, so I didn't feel like I was scuttling to keep up with him, as so often happens when walking with a much taller, longer-legged companion. I liked the small courtesies he offered too, like taking the outer edge of the sidewalk, and putting a hand under my elbow when we came to an intersection. I'm as liberated as they come, and usually hate to be treated like a piece of precious crystal, but with Dykstra these attentions seemed an unconscious reflection of how he was raised, rather than a comment on male dominance. I saw suddenly how Lelana might have genuinely cared for him, in spite of the difference in their ages or the quid pro quo that had initiated their relationship.

We turned out of my little street onto Ponce de Leon, the main artery that led from downtown Atlanta through Decatur and eventually out to the perimeter highway. As we walked, we did not talk about the Jordanian consul's call or the trip to the Bahamas. Once we were out in the crisp autumn air, walking through familiar streets, both subjects seemed unreal, and I was glad to push them out of my mind. Instead, I filled him in on the neighborhood's history. At one time, Decatur dwarfed Atlanta. But the railroad chose Atlanta, then called Terminus, as its hub, and the city grew until it swallowed its neighbor to the east. However, Decatur always remained a separate unit with its own school system, police department, courthouse and city hall. Recently, it had enjoyed a renaissance of sorts with trendy shops and sophisticated restaurants springing up around the old courthouse square.

Railroad tracks separated downtown Decatur from the leafy residential area where Agnes Scott College was located. We crossed them, and in less than fifteen minutes, we turned right into the grassy park studded with horse chestnut trees that fronted the main building, a Gothic pile trying hard to imitate Ivy League architecture. The leaves were thick on the ground, and Dykstra scuffed through them like a kid. Abruptly, he bent down to pick something up, turning away from me a little to arrange something in his hand.

"Aren't they lovely?" He presented twin chestnuts to me, glossily resting in their pulpy green coverings, as if they were a bouquet of flowers.

"Conkers." The English word leaped unbidden from my childhood. "The boys used to tie strings on them and hit them against each other in some kind of game. It's a pity they lose their shine so quickly."

"Mmm. But we have the memory." He replied cryptically. I was touched by his gesture, even if I didn't really understand its meaning. I pushed the nuts deep into my pocket, and started forward again.

"I think the refectory is around the back." I led the way along a gravel path to the right, and through a parking lot. The lot was full of cars, and a few young women were hurrying towards the main entrance, book bags over their shoulders. We soon emerged at the backside of the campus, where several modern additions abutted the early twentieth-century building. Here, there were fewer people. Eventually, we spotted the flickering yellow crime tape at the far corner of a rectangular brick building that must have housed the college commons. We headed over in silence; the memory of Lelana's death, the reason for our morning stroll, reasserted itself.

We had almost reached the small cordoned- off area when a resonant voice with a West Indian accent stopped us in our tracks.

"What is your business here?" We turned. Not six feet behind us - the sound of his approach must have been hidden by the crunch of our own footsteps – was a large black man in a security guard's uniform. Although the words were stern, his tone was gentle, even humorous. I thought they must select security personnel at this female college for their pastoral skills more than for traditional law enforcement abilities. He was even smiling.

Dykstra took the lead, indicating the crime tape.

"The girl found here was our friend. We wanted to see ….." He let his voice trail off. I sneaked a look sideways. Dykstra was looking down at the ground, his shoulders hunched and mouth compressed as if to stop tears. I couldn't tell if this was genuine emotion or intended to win the sympathy of the guard. I copied his stance.

"Oh, yes, a terrible thing to happen. I'm sorry for your loss, but you understand, there's been all kinds of TV people, rubber-neckers and that kind of thing, coming here. We have to control the area."

"Of course, we understand. Could we just have a moment? To pay our respects?" The guard nodded, and Dykstra put his hand under my arm to lead me forward. There was nothing to see really. A six-foot square of grass in the angle between a dumpster and the blank back wall of the refectory. However, we stood, heads bowed and hands clasped in front of us, as if at a graveside.

I sensed it was my turn to contribute. I turned to the guard who had approached the taped-off space along with us.

"How is the investigation progressing, Officer Little?" I read the inapposite name off the man's badge. I thought it unlikely that the police department would involve college security, at least at this man's level, but a little flattery couldn't hurt. Officer Little's chest inflated, and he seemed to grow another inch, as he replied.

"Well, you know, it's very delicate, very delicate indeed. We have to ensure the campus is completely safe. Young people, you know, are easily panicked. First thing is to find out if it happened here where the body was found."

"And? Have you been able to work that out?"

He smiled self-importantly. "We have been able to reassure the college authorities that it is extremely unlikely that the victim was killed here. A question of body heat and blood loss, that kind of thing. No, they, I mean, *we* think the time of death was some hours before she was left here."

I nodded and looked expectantly at Officer Little, employing Dobey's trick to elicit more information. But whether the guard realized he had said more than was proper, or he had nothing else to add, he remained silent, smiling sympathetically at us, and rocking back and forth on his large feet.

"Well, thanks. We'll leave now." Dykstra again took my arm. As Officer Little was struggling to extract a notebook from the chest pocket of his uniform jacket, we were already several yards away.

"Can I get your names, just for our records?" He called out.

"I'm Pieter, and she's –"

"Sally Ann." I threw the name over my shoulder, and glimpsed Officer Little studiously inscribing it into his notebook. We didn't slow our pace. Before he had a chance to ask our last names, we rounded another corner. When we regained the open area at the front of the main building, Dykstra turned to me, panting slightly from our hurried escape.

"Sally Ann?"

"My birth name." Before he could pursue it, I went on, "That wasn't very helpful, was it?"

"Maybe. At least we're narrowing the window of opportunity. You saw her on Tuesday, when? About noon?" I nodded. "And she was killed several hours before her body was found yesterday morning at five a.m. So we just have about twelve hours to account for."

I didn't see how it helped if she was killed twelve hours after I saw her, or twenty-four hours after, but he was the investigative journalist, not me. I shrugged, and we moved at a slower pace back to the main road.

"What now?"

"Two things. I think it might be useful to see what the Jordanian Consul – if it is him - wants to contact you for. And then I think you should go shopping."

I looked at him, befuddled. I was reluctant to give my contact information out to some foreign diplomat whose countryman had nearly killed me the week before, but I certainly didn't want to be shunted out of the way to the mall while Dykstra was chasing down leads. He grinned.

"A bikini? Unless you already have one, of course." He had the nerve to wink at me.

So he was really serious about me going with him on the sailing trip. I let the romantic possibilities sink in for the first time. It would be foolish of me to go with him, dangerous even. And I had work to do, responsibilities I couldn't just abandon for a week. Or could I? I was my own boss, after all, and I had no mediations scheduled until late October. I imagined the salt breeze on my face, the snap of the canvas overhead, Dykstra and me in a double berth ......

Chapter 10

We stopped off at The Dog for lunch on the way home from the college. Heather's eyes gleamed when I walked in with a man other than Gerardo. She seized a couple of menus, and, ignoring a customer's outstretched coffee cup, raced us to one of the booths.

"Well, hiya, Sarah. Nice to see you!" She looked meaningfully from me to Dykstra. I was enjoying resisting her desperate need to be introduced to him.

"Good to see you too, Heather. What's good today?"

She gave a tinkling laugh, and flirted her eyes between me and Dykstra. "Everything's good! Just depends what you're in the mood for." She leant forward to point out the specials, treating him to a close-up of her cleavage. "So, Saul does a mean spaghetti *con vongole*, if you're a shellfish man, or there's the ever-popular soup 'n' salad. Today's soup *du jour* is tomato and roasted red pepper."

She stood there for a moment, smiling brightly, but Dykstra continued to scan the menu.

"O.K. I'll leave you two to think about it." She rolled her eyes at me, and swished back to the counter.

Dykstra, noting my amusement, raised his eyebrows.

"She likes to think she knows all about me, but I've stumped her by coming in here with a tall, good-looking stranger."

"Do you want me to play along? Should I look deep into your eyes?"

I started to laugh, then thought of him and Lelana, and the smoldering looks they had exchanged the night I first saw them.

"Better not." I changed the subject. "She's right about the spaghetti, and the sandwiches are good too." It was my turn to hide behind the menu.

We ordered, and made inconsequential conversation until our food arrived. Before Heather left, Dykstra finally rewarded her with one of his most boyish smiles. Then he leaned forward and spoke quietly to me.

"Why don't we find out the number of the Jordanian Embassy, and you call the Consul yourself, rather than giving the detective permission to release your number? That way, you can be sure you're speaking to him, not an imposter."

"That makes sense," I responded. "Is there anything we can find out from him? I mean, would *he* know about the smuggling scheme? He might even be part of it. If Jordanian government officials are involved, they might use their embassy people. After all, can't diplomats get stuff across borders without being searched? "

"That's true, but I didn't find any link to Jordanians. Lebanon, Egypt, Syria: these are the countries with the most corruption, the most autocratic governments, and therefore the biggest risk of being overthrown. Their leaders are nervous. Right now, Jordan's stable and fairly democratic in comparison. The Consul might still help us with some background on Lelana's family, though. It might let us understand her connection better."

We tossed around the possibilities for a while: what questions I should ask, whether Dykstra should participate in the conversation, and how much I should reveal about the sphinx. That led to us comparing interview techniques. There was not that much daylight between how an investigative reporter approaches a witness and how a mediator teases out a party's position.

"This can't be the only story you're working on. What am I going to read about next?"

"Actually, yes, this *is* the only story I'm working on. I'm lucky that I can focus like this. Europ News has stringers in every country. They wire in stories all the time, and different outlets – TV, newspapers – pick them up … or not. Bureau chiefs like me can choose which ones to follow up on, which ones are worth more than a single day's headlines, and then dig deeper. I've been chasing this hidden assets thing around the Middle East for months."

Which explained why his London flat had that movie-set, unlived-in feel: he was never there. I wanted to ask some more personal questions: had he ever been married? But I was still nervous about probing too deeply, in case he wanted similar revelations from me. I wasn't ready for that.

We wrestled briefly over the check before I let him pay. ("Expenses!" he crowed.) I left a tip on the table then followed him to the cash register where Heather was at last basking his full attention.

"Enjoy your time in Atlanta!" She trilled, as Dykstra stepped ahead of me to open the door. I caught Heather's eye. She was shaking her fingers as if she had been burned, and mouthing "So hot!" For the second day in a row, I left The Dog with a smile on my face. Yesterday, it was the result of healthy exercise; today it was all Dykstra. I had had misgivings about going to The Dog: out-in-public together, not a date, but kind of a milestone. I was pleased with how it went. We were getting more and more comfortable with each other.

Back at the house, it needed only a few keystrokes to discover the number for Jordan's Consul General in Washington

DC. However, it took much longer to penetrate the layers of embassy underlings before I got through to the man himself.

"This is Sarah McKinney. I'm calling about Lelana Sherat. She was murdered in Atlanta yesterday," I repeated for the umpteenth time. I was answered by an aristocratic British accent, no doubt the product of some very expensive public school.

"This is Mahmet Barouk, Consul General. Thank you so much for calling me. I understand Miss Sherat came to see you on Tuesday. Is that correct?"

Wait a minute. Hadn't Detective Dobey said he wasn't going to give out my name until I gave permission? Barouk must have put two and two together himself, or possibly leaned on Dobey's superiors for information. I refused to be put on the defensive.

"Is the Embassy doing its own investigation into her murder then?" I had the phone on speaker so Dykstra could listen in. He gave me an approving nod.

"No, no, we leave all that to the local police," Barouk seemed in a hurry to reassure me. "It's just that Ms. Sherat's father wanted to talk to you. He'll be coming to Atlanta to collect the, er, body." His voiced dropped as if embarrassed to refer to the fact of her death.

"Why does he want to talk to me? I hardly knew her."

"Well, you see, it's a little delicate .... Mr. Sherat and his daughter had become estranged over the last few months. He just wants to find out how she seemed, was she happy, that sort of thing."

"Really." I thought it was unlikely that the Consulate provided this service for all Jordanian next of kin whose family members died on US soil. I let my response hang.

"Well, as I said, it's a little delicate. Mr. Sherat is a former minister in the Jordanian government. He is still very well respected in my country, you see. We want to help him find ....

closure." Barouk said the word "closure" as if it smelled bad. I sensed that, if he had leaned on the Decatur PD, someone else was leaning on him and he didn't like it, but he soldiered on. "Yes, and you may also be able to help him locate another friend of Miss Sherat's, a journalist based in London called Pieter Dykstra."

I looked inquiringly at Dykstra, waiting for an indication from him on how to proceed. Instead, Dykstra jumped in himself.

"This is Pieter Dykstra. And how may I help Mr. Sherat find … closure?"

The Consul recovered quickly from this surprising intervention.

"Ah, Mr. Dykstra. Well, this is fortunate. I am, of course, familiar with your work for the news agency. So you and Miss McKinney are friends too?"

Dykstra ignored the question. "I'm aware of the estrangement between Lelana and her father, and I expect he blames me for it, so why would he want to talk to me?"

"I really can't tell you any more than I've already explained. Mr. Sherat regrets that he wasn't closer to his daughter before her … umm, in the last few months. He wants to be assured that she was alright, well-cared for, that sort of thing."

"She was murdered. Clearly, she wasn't being 'well-cared for.'" Dykstra's voice was as sharp and thin as a knife blade.

"Look. Mr. Sherat arrives in DC tomorrow and flies to Atlanta on Saturday morning. Can you both meet him or not?" The public school veneer of casual good manners was wearing thin. The diplomat wanted this conversation to be over.

Dykstra and I exchanged looks. He was silently soliciting my opinion. I nodded more decisively than I felt.

"OK, we'll meet Mr. Sherat at the Atlanta airport. What time does his flight get in?"

"I'll call you back to let you know, and where to meet him. Thank you both, and good bye."

I pressed disconnect, and let out my breath.

"What do you think? Is Lelana's father just looking for 'closure'?" I mimicked the Consul's distaste for the word.

Dykstra was jubilant. "Who knows? But this gets us closer. We'll find out what *he* knows about Lelana's involvement, and possibly why she was killed. Sherat is no longer in power, but he's close to power. It would take Dobey years to get access to the kind of information Sherat can get to with a single phone call."

Dykstra was thumbing through e-mails on his smartphone.

"This is convenient. What's the closest airport to, er, Hilton Head?"

"Hilton Head's in South Carolina, on the coast. I guess the nearest airport's Savannah. Why?" I had never been to Hilton Head, a millionaires' enclave on a coastal island. Gated communities for the super-rich. Golf and game fishing, not my scene, although I imagined some of the corporate bigwigs who retained my services might have vacation homes on the island.

"Arun says the yacht's berthed there. He says, 'Leaving port Saturday night. Confirm you'll be there.' We could fly to Savannah after we meet with Lelana's father."

"Hey, wait a minute. I can't just leave everything." But I could, I could. And I wanted to, more than anything. It wasn't just being with Dykstra, although already I felt a growing connection, much more than the physical attraction that had plagued me since I first saw him. It was the adventure, something new and challenging that would take me beyond the limits of my laboriously carved-out life, the safety of isolation and neutrality. Dykstra knew it; he knew I'd go with him. He didn't pressure me, argue with me, try to seduce me with his eyes, his voice. He just sat and looked at me, waiting for me to say – inevitably – yes!

***

Saturday morning, Atlanta-Hartsfield-Jackson Airport was not particularly busy. Not busy, that is, compared to weekdays, when hundreds of thousands of business travelers churned through, fighting automatic check-in machines, surly porters and bitter airline ticket agents. Even so, the Starbucks where we whiled away a half-hour waiting for Lelana's father's plane, was littered with crumbs and crumpled napkins. Barouk's secretary had called with the details. Mr. Sherat was arriving on the Delta shuttle from Washington DC at 10.15 am. A room had been reserved at the Delta Sky Lounge on Terminal T. We would be escorted through Security by an airport official at exactly 10.10 am. We had not shared the information that our flight for Savannah left at noon, and we already had the boarding passes that would allow us to pass through Security without escort.

Dykstra had picked me up from my house in a taxi early that morning. When, on Thursday afternoon, he announced that he'd found a hotel room, I couldn't disguise my sudden and unreasonable disappointment. He immediately picked up on it, and took a step forward, hand outstretched.

"Sarah —"

I gathered myself quickly together. "No, of course. I mean, you're welcome to stay, but your back must be killing you. That sofa's not very comfortable. Can I give you a ride?" I turned away and scanned the room distractedly to avoid looking at him.

"Sarah, it's just I think we need time, *I* need time ...." He trailed off. *OK, Sarah, this is where you always screw it up, where you close down your emotions and throw some cynical comment back. Just for once, can you allow yourself to be vulnerable?*

I took a deep breath. "I understand. You're right." I finally forced myself to meet his eye. "I'm not good at relationships, never have been.... ."

He smiled, took my hand and raised it to his lips, the gesture was both courtly and intimate. I smiled back, astonished to feel tears pricking my eyelids. Dykstra continued to hold my hand, now softly stroking my palm with his thumb. He spoke slowly, the trace of an accent accentuated. "I hope this is a new start ….. for both of us."

That night and the next, I relived the exchange a hundred times, tossing and turning alone in my bed, at one moment exultant, planning a future with Dykstra, the next neurotically afraid that I had fooled myself into trusting a man I hardly knew. In the light of the intervening day, I was able to distract myself with work, packing for the trip, and preparing the house for another absence.   I even remembered to call Gerardo and warn him I'd be away for a few days. I confirmed that the dead girl was Lelana.

"Who kill her? The big man?" Gerardo did not like phone conversations. He was embarrassed about his English.

"I don't know, Gerardo. The police are looking for him. " I waited while he put together his next question.

"Is same man who broke door?"

"It may be connected." Another pause.

"Sarah, you be careful please." This time it was me who could not find the words. I blinked back sudden tears and swallowed hard.

"Thank you."

"*De nada.*" He hung up. I stood for a while with the phone to my ear, listening to the echo of his gruff affection reverberate in my heart.

***

Although I enjoy the experience of flying itself – the liberation of piercing the clouds and freeing myself from the demands of my day-to-day existence – I hate airports. Since 9/11, paranoia has stripped whatever romance was left to the preparatory phase of slipping the bounds of earth. The extra fees for bags, food, and an assigned seat compounded the insult. I wondered when there would be an extra charge for using the bathroom, maybe breathing. But wealth and power still have their privileges. Once we had linked up with the Atlanta Airport official charged with our conduct, we passed through Security effortlessly, and in a matter of minutes were installed (with far superior coffee) in a glass-walled conference room in Delta's most luxurious first class lounge. One wall was glass, with a view over the taxi-ways so we could watch the parade of jets perform their slow do-si-do, some heading for the terminal gates, others crawling out to the runway for take-off. The glass must have been thick; their engine noise was reduced to a polite hum.

At exactly 10.20, a tall slim gentleman entered the room, accompanied by a shorter, stouter individual in a cheap suit. Without a word, the gentleman nodded brusquely to us, and indicated that his companion should withdraw. Shrugging off the camel-hair coat draped over his shoulders, he then sat down at the head of the table, steepling his hands and looking over them at Dykstra with a piercing stare. We took our seats side by side with our backs to the view.

The silence stretched for several seconds. I took the opportunity to note the family resemblance. Lelana's father had bequeathed her his tall rangey build. His dark hair, worn a little longer than current fashion – a sign of vanity perhaps? - was barely touched with silvery streaks. His face was carved with vertical lines: between his eyebrows, and from nose to mouth to chin. They exaggerated his thinness, and made him look older than the fifty-something I guessed him to be. His eyes glowed black. His suit was conservative and well-tailored. I had expected a fundamentalist Muslim to wear a turban or other form of traditional dress, but this man could pass for a Wall Street banker or Los Angeles doctor.

"Mr. Dykstra, tell me about my daughter." It was a command from a man accustomed to power. Clearly, introductions and other social niceties were deemed unnecessary.

"What do you want to know? She came to London with me because she didn't want the marriage you had arranged for her. I looked after her as best I could." Here, he squeezed my hand under the table, "I thought she was happy. Then, about ten days ago, a man tried to kill her. He missed, thanks to Miss McKinney, here." Another squeeze. "The bullet hit Sarah instead. Then, a few days later, Lelana left without warning or explanation. Next thing, she's in Atlanta, dead."

"And you don't know why?" There was a sneer in the older man's voice.

"Do *you*? Who sent the gunman to kill her in the restaurant? There was a woman in a burkah with him. Your sister?" Dykstra kept his voice level, but there was a definite challenge in his words.

"No! She would never –" Lelana's father reared back in his seat as if he had been struck in the face.

"Are you sure?"

For the first time, I felt a twinge of sympathy for Mr. Sherat. He had, after all, lost his wife and now his daughter. I wanted to hear his side of things, so, although he had pointedly ignored me since entering the room, I interjected a question, trying to make my tone unthreatening.

"The man Lelana was supposed to marry? What do you know about him? Do you think he might have wished to harm her after she escaped from him?"

Mr. Sherat met my eye reluctantly. "I know his family. It is honorable. I understood the man to be devout. I have not met him." I carefully suppressed any sign of shock that a father would give his daughter to a man he had not met. "I leave domestic arrangements to the women. Had I known that this marriage was so distasteful to Lelana, of course, I would not have forced her into it."

"Did you discuss it with her? Did you ask her what she wanted?" Dykstra was getting more aggressive, the cool reporter losing out to the bereaved lover.

"Mr. Dykstra, you cannot understand our customs and tradition. Marriages have been successfully arranged between families for generations. My own marriage, which was very happy, was arranged by my father."

Dykstra broke into what I guessed was Arabic. He started slowly and quietly, but gradually became more forceful. When he finished, the two men stared at each other. Sherat was the first to break eye contact. He nodded twice, and said something in Arabic before reverting to English.

"If I am at fault, it was to allow Lelana too much freedom. My wife insisted that Lelana needed to experience the world before she settled down in marriage. They were close. After my wife died, she wouldn't listen to anyone. It was too late." There was little of the former arrogance left in his tone of voice.

"Who were her friends? How was she spending her time?" Dykstra resumed his journalist persona, speaking now in a carefully neutral tone.

Sherat shrugged helplessly. "I don't know."

"Did you know she was involved with Hammet Kahn's son?" Dykstra had told me that this was the boyfriend arrested for drug smuggling in Turkey.

"I don't believe it! That boy brought disgrace to his family. My daughter would never –" A sudden flair of self-righteousness revived Sherat, but Dykstra was relentless.

"We think she was involved with people smuggling other things too, illegal diamonds from West Africa, for example. People working for highly placed officials in Middle East countries. What do you know about this?"

"You are crazy!" But I could see Lelana's father was coming to understand a new picture of his daughter. Whatever Dykstra had said to him in Arabic had hit home. His posture was no longer erect, and his previously steely glare was now a confused gaze shifting from object to object around the conference room, as if looking for the key to a riddle.

I intervened again. "Look, we want to find whoever killed Lelana. It might have something to do with the smuggling ring, or it might be an honor killing: Lelana's fiancé or someone he hired might have gone after her. Will you help us?"

"I know nothing about this smuggling, or other criminal activity! My government service was impeccable; my colleagues too —"

"We're not accusing you or the Jordanian government. But perhaps you have access to information about other governments in the region? At least, you could satisfy yourself that she wasn't killed because she ran away from an arranged marriage. I think you'd want to do that, Mr. Sherat?"

Again, I could see it took an effort to meet my eye. In his world, a woman should not be suggesting a course of action to him. He saved face by responding to Dykstra.

"I will naturally make sure that no one in my family, or the family with whom I intended the alliance has had a hand in my daughter's death. I think you overestimate my access and influence in government circles, especially outside Jordan, but if I learn of anything material about this so-called smuggling I shall let you know. You have a card?"

Dykstra stood to exchange business cards with Lelana's father. The ceremony of this mundane act seemed to give the older man a new backbone. He rose to his feet, and arranged his overcoat over his shoulders with care.

"Lelana will be buried in Amman tomorrow night. *Ma'a salama.*" Without looking at either of us again, he walked steadily

97

to the door, opened it to reveal his companion in the act of jumping away, and left.

"Poor man." In spite of his stiffness and his refusal to acknowledge me, I felt sorry for Lelana's misguided father. Dykstra clearly did not share my feelings. He was scowling down at the card Sherat had given him. "What did you say to him?"

"I told him that I had been raised in a Muslim country, that I fully understood his customs and traditions, and that I hoped he would be able to live with the knowledge that those customs and traditions led to his daughter running away and perhaps to her death. She deserved a better father." He looked up, shaking off his bleak mood. "Come on, let's find our flight to Savannah."

Chapter 11

It was at least ten degrees warmer on the coast than in Atlanta, and the palmettos and scrubby pines that lined the quiet avenues on Hilton Head Island showed no sign of the changing season. The plantation-style mansions set back from the road made me feel as if carried back to an earlier time, the fifties maybe, when conflict, foreign or domestic, could be safely hidden behind a leisurely lifestyle of tennis at ten and cocktails at six. Provided, of course, that you had the money.

The Sea Pines Resort shuttle van transported us and another couple from Savannah Airport to the southwest tip of the island where the motor yacht *Glissando* was berthed in the Sea Pines marina. I felt good sitting next to Dykstra, our thighs touching, just another vacationing twosome. On the short flight down we had swapped awful flight stories. He won the contest hands down, and made my stomach ache with laughter from his description of an Air Yemeni flight from Aden to Khartoum, an Australian pilot high on hashish, and a cargo bay full of stolen Israeli munitions. He had managed to quell my misgivings about the trip at least for the present.

Our fellow travelers were a pair of healthy retirees, tanned and well-dressed in Ralph Lauren casuals. She volunteered that they were from Chicago, here for a long weekend of golf before traveling on to their daughter's home in Atlanta. Her husband, once he ascertained that we were not here for the golf, was content to let her chatter on. And we were content to listen, Dykstra's hand resting on mine. She required no more than the occasional affirming nod or smile from us as she commented on the shops and restaurants she planned to visit, the people they had met on the plane, the son-in-law's banking job, the grandchildren's private school. If it were not for a reproving glance from her husband, I think she would have gone on to reveal the intimacies of her daughter's marriage and their own current income level, but she lapsed into silence as we cruised through the resort's main security gates. Soon after, the van stopped at their hotel.

"It was so lovely to meet you. I do hope we see you again while we're here," she gushed while her husband assembled their luggage and tipped the driver. "Bye-ee!"

As she skipped lightly down the van's steps, the man looked ruefully back at us, and gave the slightest shrug. Dykstra and I, still wrapped in our cocoon of coupledom, smiled back at him sympathetically.

Within another five minutes we were at the marina. Our driver explained that we could find our vessel by inquiring at the marina office. However, any such inquiry was unnecessary. As soon as the shuttle van pulled away from the curb, we spotted the *Glissando*. It was impossible to miss: the largest yacht in the marina, too long for the closer side-by-side slips, it had the entire outer arm of the harbor wall to itself.

"My God, she must be twenty-five meters long!" Dykstra was impressed in spite of himself. All I could say was "Wow!" My Puritan streak abhorred the conspicuous consumption, while my inner deprived child was yearning to experience the luxury. We stood there for a moment, our bags at our feet, taking in the yacht's gleaming white superstructure. There were decks fore and aft, separated by at least forty feet of staterooms. The enclosed flying bridge atop the structure bristled with radio antennae and other high tech equipment. Even the inflatable tender on hoists at the stern was probably large enough to accommodate eight comfortably. I counted a dozen portholes below the deck line, and tried to guess how many cabins that might equate to.

"Well, shall we go aboard?" Dykstra was grinning at me, as he hoisted his duffel bag, and grabbed my little roll-on. He led the way along the boardwalk that skirted the marina.

"Who did your pal say owns this boat?"

"*Yacht,* Sarah, not boat," he teased. "I'm not really sure. Arun said something about 'a consortium.' His father's a banker, which means he's a specialist in clever ownership arrangements. There's probably a shell corporation owned by another shell corporation with a registered office in Switzerland or something."

By this time we had reached the outer arm of the marina where the *Glissando* was moored. I could see the name on the stern and, underneath, that it was registered in Freeport in the Bahamas. As we approached, a slim young man, with sun-bleached hair and a deep tan, emerged through the double doors from the stateroom. He was wearing neatly pressed jeans and a coral-colored polo shirt with the yacht's name on the right side of his chest. He was barefoot.

"Can I help you?" His smile revealed perfect white teeth.

"We're guests of Arun El-Bared. Has he arrived yet?"

"You must be Mr. Dykstra and ... er, friend?" I didn't care for the way this crew member, as I guessed him to be, looked me over, his expensive orthodonture still on show, but I restrained myself from reacting. "Mr. El-Bared and Mr. Yusef have gone over to Salty Dan's for cocktails. He asked me to settle you in, then direct you there to join them. I believe they have a table reserved for dinner." He gestured vaguely behind us at the parade of expensive shops and restaurants that lined the marina.

Ignoring his proffered hand, I stepped quickly across the gangplank and onto the glossy decking, Dykstra following with our luggage.

"This way. By the way, I'm Steve – Captain Steve, actually." He relieved Dykstra of the bags, smiling in an ingratiating way that instilled no particular faith in his navigational skills. I raised my eyebrows at Dykstra as we fell in line behind him. Dykstra mockingly saluted and mouthed *Aye aye, Cap'n* at Steve's retreating back.

Steve led us into the first of a suite of above-deck staterooms. We were in what he explained was the 'day cabin': invitingly cushioned sofas upholstered in pale mushroom suede lined the bulkheads. Everything was glass above them, and we didn't even have to duck to take in the vista of the other yachts in the marina and the commercial buildings beyond, their windows reflecting the sun. An ice bucket housing an open bottle of Dom Perignon was centered on a steel and glass coffee table, next to a vase of two dozen casually arranged tulips, the exact same shade as Steve's shirt.

"Please, help yourselves." Steve indicated the champagne. I thought about how much out of season tulips cost; they must have been flown in from some place in the Southern hemisphere where it was now spring. Not to mention the sad waste of bubbles in undrunk champagne.

"We'll pass for now." Dykstra and I again exchanged glances, communicating our shared amazement at the sumptuousness of the decor.

Steve was already opening another set of double doors to the room beyond. "Dining room – galley's through those doors; there's a head through there – that's what we call the bathroom on ship," he added coyly.

"Really." I made my voice sweet, but with a hint of *don't patronize me, buster.*

"This is the saloon." A smaller stateroom decorated in a clubby style with a dark leather sofa, a sixty-inch flat screen television, and a built-in drinks cabinet that lurked like Sasquatch in a corner.

"Through there is the master bedroom. I'll just let you have a peek. That's where Mr. Tanello and his … guest will be sleeping." The same suggestive hesitation as when he had referred to me as Dykstra's "….friend." He held the door ajar so I could look through.

"And who is Mr. Tanello?" Dykstra made it sound like an idle question, as he looked over the titles of obviously unread volumes arranged just so on a side table in the saloon.

"Oh, he's Mr. El-Bared's friend?" Captain Steve put a query in his voice. He was clearly surprised we did not know Tanello, and were not awed by the mere mention of his name.

"Of course. Wall Street type, isn't he?" Dykstra kept it casual, peering over my shoulder into the lavish stateroom beyond. The natural materials and muted tones of the rooms we had passed through so far were replaced here by what I could only call Vegas whore's boudoir style. The king-sized bed was draped with a leopard skin over burgundy velvet. The carpet was thick cream shag. Although the blinds in this room were tightly drawn, the rosy light dispensed by silk-shaded wall sconces revealed a painting of a voluptuous nude in the style of Renoir. No, it *was* a Renoir: I could just make out the familiar signature at the bottom right of the picture.

"Well, I think Mr. Tanello has a finger in a number of pies." Steve said archly, as he closed the door to the master suite. "Now, let me take you below to your quarters."

Back in the day cabin were twin stairways to the lower deck. We descended the one to the left – "This is the port companionway" Steve announced – and found ourselves in a corridor that crossed the yacht from one side to the other. On each side were two doors, two leading aft and two leading forward. Steve opened the first door leading aft.

"Each cabin has its own head, including shower. There's a double berth in each." He smirked. "So, the two aft cabins are made up and ready. Mr. El-Bared and Mr. Yusef are in the two forward cabins. Crew quarters are up in the bow beyond theirs. Shall I bring both your bags in here?" The smirk was becoming irritating.

We had not previously discussed sleeping arrangements. "Will you take this one or the starboard cabin, darling?" I affected a film star drawl to hide my nervousness.

"Whichever you like. " Dykstra strolled past Steve to open the door to the other aft cabin. "They're identical." I didn't know whether to be relieved or disappointed at his calm acceptance of separate quarters.

Once Steve had deposited my bag, I quickly peeled off the sweater that had been appropriate for Atlanta, but was much too warm now. I shook out a white silk shirt, determined that it was not too creased to wear, and substituted Chacos for the cowboy boots I had traveled in. The black jeans I was wearing would do for any climate or occasion. Then I bent forward, letting my shoulder length hair fall towards the floor. I spritzed it with hair spray, and stood to finger-style it back into life. A quick refresh of my make-up, and I was ready to face the world again.

Dykstra had spent the brief downtime doing a search on his smart phone for information about the mysterious Mr. Tanello who had so powerfully impressed Captain Steve and was to be accorded the best accommodations on the yacht. He had been frustrated to find nothing relevant, and so had searched the *Glissando*'s registration information instead. Another dead-end: as he suspected, all inquiries were directed to an offshore bank in the Grand Caymans. He told me the results of his searches as we strolled over to Salty Dan's, a bar-restaurant at the furthest end of the marina, with the best view of what was developing into a spectacular sunset. A chorus line of pelicans was silhouetted against a broad silver path leading across the water to the southwestern horizon. The sky was painted with sweeping strokes of orange and crimson and streaked with a light mesh of pale pink cirrus. As if directed by some invisible stage manager, a shrimp boat slowly traversed the sun's reflected path, black spider arms extended. I wanted to linger outside and enjoy the show, breathing in the smell of the sea, but instead reluctantly turned away to precede Dykstra into the noisy bar.

Dykstra had clued me in on the flight down that Arun and Paul, once away from the strict standards of their homelands, were heavy drinkers. I should expect them to be indulging their taste for alcohol at every opportunity on this trip. In fact, Dykstra was counting on this, as their drinking would make it more likely that they would let slip information useful to the investigation. So I was not surprised to see an assembly of glasses on their table, empty but for melting ice cubes and crumpled little paper umbrellas. What did surprise me was the youth of the two men – just boys, really - who were our hosts. They both had neatly trimmed dark hair and smooth complexions. Arun was distinguishable by a pronounced Adam's apple, and Paul was a little plumper; otherwise it was hard to tell them apart. They wore the classless uniform of young men everywhere: stone-washed jeans, Nikes, and body-hugging hoodies, Arun's was grey, Paul's dark blue. The only signs of their wealth were the diamond-studded Tag Hauer watches on their wrists and the gold chain that escaped the neck of Paul's hoodie.

They stood somewhat unsteadily as I was introduced, and spoke over each other to say how pleased they were to meet me. Seated again, Paul turned away to attract the attention of a server, while Arun grasped Dykstra's arm and looked soulfully into his eyes.

"Man, I'm so sorry, you know, about Lelana. It's terrible. What can I say? I just can't believe it. She was so beautiful, so

105

….." He shook his head to demonstrate his disbelief, and reached for his glass. Finding it empty, he too started scanning the room for a waitress to take an order for another round. His idioms were American, but his accent, though slurred, was British public school, like the Jordanian consul who had set up the meeting with Lelana's father.

We ordered drinks. Paul took his turn at commiserating with Dykstra over Lelana's death. I sipped my white wine, happy to just observe the conversation. Unlike Mr. Sherat, whose disdain was motivated by religion, culture and politics, Arun and Paul just seemed shy around women. In spite of their wealth and international education, they were unused to talking to a professional older female, and my few casually inserted questions were greeted with embarrassed downward smiles and hesitant replies.

Dykstra encouraged the party to move on to the restaurant, thinking, no doubt, that food would soak up some of the excess alcohol. Eventually, the bar tab was settled, and, with Paul and Arun leaning on each other for support, he led the way through to our reserved table. I brought up the rear.

The serving staff was garbed in a cheesy take-off of a French matelot's uniform: striped jerseys and polyester bell-bottoms. The food was eclectic. Our waitress was professionally cheerful, and very loud. She handed us menus as large as laminated bedsheets.

"Something for everyone!" She yelled. Dykstra and I split a bottle of Argentinian Malbec, but Arun and Paul continued to order the sticky rum drinks that were touted as Salty Dan's specialty. I had overcooked scallops, Dykstra had a tough steak, and the boys ordered paella, but only ate the rice. They alternated between noisy reminiscences of places and people in the Middle East, and exaggeratedly reverential references to Lelana. Paul had been her childhood playmate. Arun had known her "for ages." I participated little in the conversation. Dykstra held his end up well, eventually guiding the conversation back to the present and the mystery guest, Mr. Tanello.

"He's a ver' important man. Ver' well-connected. His organization ...." Arun broke off to sweep his arms around in a gesture demonstrating how important and well-connected Tanello was, knocking over a water glass in the process. "He's a fixer. You want something done, he does it. I don't mean World Cup tickets. I mean, like, the top guys, they all go to him. Not just in the US, I mean *everywhere*."

"So, is he a banker? A financial advisor? Where is he based?" Dykstra probed.

"Yes! He's a banker – a private banker." Arun put his finger alongside his nose in the universally understood signal. "He's a ver' *private* banker! And he's based *everywhere*, man. I told you!"

Paul leaned forward. "The yacht, the *Glissando,* that's his, and he has a place in Monte Carlo and London, and New York, of course, and his own jet, and ...." He gave up, exhausted by the effort of listing all Tanello's assets, and sat nodding wisely.

"So the *Glissando* belongs to Mr. Tanello? That's interesting. Why does he want us along on this trip? I've never met the guy." Dykstra's voice was deceptively casual; he was even slurring his words a little to keep the boys company.

"No, it's Lelana he wanted – Oh, I didn't mean, I shouldn't have said ...."Arun floundered around for a moment, then looked earnestly at Dykstra. "Truth is, you were invited just as Lelana's guest. Tanello wanted to meet her and you were together, so .... He knows Lelana's dead, and I've told him you're bringing someone else. He's cool with it. I told him you knew Lelana, too," A brief grin in my direction.

"How did you know Sarah knew Lelana?" Dykstra asked, his voice cool. I think I was the only one to hear the edge in it.

"Wha...? I guess Lelana told me. Yeah, she mus' have told me. You know, after you ... . Look, I can't remember, OK?" Arun was now angry, with the sudden change of mood that sometimes happens with drunks.

"We need to get back to the yacht. Mr.Tanello-- Lou's probably arrived." Paul changed the subject, visibly pulling himself together, and signaling for the bill. I was glad the meal was over. There was an awkward silence, as Arun sulkily played with the remaining food on his plate and Paul felt through his pockets for his wallet. Dykstra and I sat quiet as church mice, processing the evening's information.

Night had fallen while we were eating. There was no moon, and the light posts around the marina left pools of darkness in between, where Arun and Paul stumbled against each other. As we neared the *Glissando*, we heard raised voices from the stern deck, and saw two figures outlined against the interior lights.

"I signed on for the season! You can't just—" It was Steve's voice. He sounded somewhere between plaintive and pissed off. A deeper voice responded; I couldn't make out the words. Our party reached the shore-side of the gangplank, just as Steve reached the ship-side end. He locked eyes with Arun, who had already taken a step forward onto the walkway. Confused, Arun reared back, knocking Paul to the side. Steve strode across, casting a baleful look at each of us as he passed.

"What's going on?" Dykstra's question went unanswered. Arun and Paul shambled forward onto the deck. We hung back. A man was standing just outside the open double doors to the day cabin, his hands in the pockets of his chinos. He was wearing a Hawaian shirt in shades of cream and aqua. It drew attention away from his face, which was in any case an ordinary face, neither plain nor handsome, an unexceptional face, topped with mousy hair. I had no reason to feel fear, but nevertheless a shiver ran down my spine, and I gripped Dykstra's hand tight.

"Arun! Paul! Great to see you. Slight change of plan. We have a new captain." I don't think Tanello had noticed Dykstra and me yet, still at the gloomy end of the gangplank. "This is Marco; he's very skilled."

Tanello turned to the lighted day cabin, gesturing for whoever was inside to come out. Then he spotted us and approached with hand outstretched.

"Well, this is a pleasure! Pieter Dykstra, I assume? And this is....?"

Dykstra stepped forward to shake Tanello's hand and introduce me. At the same moment, I recognized the man emerging from the day cabin. I ducked my head into Dykstra's chest, sliding my hand round his waist and pinching hard at the flesh above his belt. I was feigning tipsy, hoping Dykstra would play along.

"That man, the new captain," I whispered furiously into Dykstra's shirt. "That's the man with Lelana when she came to my house last Tuesday."

Chapter 12

If Steve seemed somehow lightweight for the role of captain on a seagoing yacht like the *Glissando*, Marco was definitely in a heavier weight class. His muscles bulged through a tight black t-shirt, and his hands hung like small hams at his side. When I had first seen him standing in my driveway several days earlier, I thought he looked like a gangster, and that impression was renewed as he stood impassively behind Tanello. His dark eyes were hooded, and his mouth set in a hard line. He acknowledged Tanello's introduction with a scant one-inch inclination of the head. He gave no sign that he recognized me.

Arun and Paul dropped gratefully into the plush sofas that lined the day cabin, talking over each other in their rush to compliment Tanello ("Just call me Lou, please!") on the beauty of his yacht. Dykstra and I remained quiet. I slouched a little, cultivating my cover as having drunk too much, but I could feel an electric current vibrating in Dykstra, who sat upright like a well-trained hunting dog on the scent. Tanello remained standing with a slight smile on his face, looking down from one of us to the other, as if sizing up a potential purchase.

Arun and Paul fell silent as the door to the inner stateroom opened. The woman who emerged had white-blond hair that hung straight to her impressive breasts. Their size was out of proportion to the rest of her stick-like frame. She had pale blue eyes that gave her a disturbingly vacant look, exaggerated by the way her mouth hung slightly open. Her lips, like her breasts, were artificially enhanced. She was wearing a skin-tight zebra print top and a short, equally tight black skirt. Somewhere in the recesses of my brain I held the memory that high heels were *verboten* on deck. If so, she had been granted an exemption: her black strappy sandals had five inch stilettos as narrow and sharp as the blade they were named for. This must be Tanello's date. Dykstra and I exchanged the briefest of glances, just enough to flash the shared perception: she was a hooker.

"Ingrid, honey, come and meet my guests."

Although her name and coloring were Swedish, Ingrid's accent was pure New Jersey.

"Pleased ta meetcha." She matched Marco for impassivity. Without extending a hand or cracking a smile, she sank into a corner of the sofa, and stared out into the night.

"Champagne?" Tanello gestured to the bottle in the ice bucket. I wondered if it was the same one opened by Steve hours before. If so, it must be flat by now. Only Ingrid indicated acceptance, and Tanello poured her a glass with a flourish, then sat down next to her, his hand on her thigh. Marco was the only one standing, guarding the exit with his arms folded over well-developed pectoral muscles.

"Well!" Tanello continued to smile. If it were not for his brightly colored shirt, Tanello would be difficult to pick out in a crowd: average height, average build, clean-shaven, no discernable accent. And yet he managed to dominate the space. I suppose that was because he literally owned it. He seemed quite comfortable as the silence extended, but Paul and Arun shifted nervously on the cushions. I could sense their need to fill the void, at the same time realizing that they might be too drunk to make a sensible contribution. Eventually, silence squeezing them like a vise, they burst into speech at the same time.

"So what's the plan, Lou?"

"When do we set sail?"

"The plan? Just as I told you on the phone, we'll make a straight run down to Freeport on Grand Bahama, then take our time island-hopping down the chain to, oh, say, Deadman's Cay?" He laughed softly."It'll be great. We're just waiting on another crew member to arrive. As soon as he gets here, we'll leave harbor."

Paul failed to suppress a yawn, and murmured "jetlag" sheepishly.

"My apologies, you must all be exhausted. There's no need to wait up. I'm not sure when our missing crew member will arrive, so I insist you all get some rest. We'll have plenty of time to talk later." His smile was becoming unnerving. Although his manners were perfect and his voice pleasantly modulated, I couldn't wait to get out of his presence. It bothered me that he might know more about me than I did about him. That, and the fact that Dykstra and I were apparently here at *his* command, not just the random invitees of the spoiled rich kids who were now stumbling through their goodnights and toward the stairway to below decks. I hated that loss of control. I had managed to convince myself that I could play detective with Dykstra *and* get an expenses-paid Caribbean vacation at the same time. But Tanello had orchestrated our presence for his own private reasons, and very soon now we would be on the high seas completely at his mercy.

Dykstra stood up and turned to extend a hand to me, but he spoke to Tanello.

"Goodnight then, and thanks so much for inviting me on this cruise. I know Lelana was looking forward to seeing you again."

"Lelana? We never met, I'm sorry to say. Arun told me about her. I imagine it was a huge loss. My sympathies." He modified his smile to demonstrate his sincerity.

I murmured my goodnights, receiving a response only from Tanello, and made my way to the port stairway, while Dykstra rather ostentatiously took the starboard one. A last glance over my shoulder revealed the three of them, Ingrid still staring out at the blackness, Marco like a piece of rough-hewn granite by the exterior doors, and Tanello, motionless between them, his Cheshire cat grin slowly fading as I descended below decks.

I sat on my bunk taking deep breaths. Within a minute, there was a soft tap on the door.

"Sarah? It's me."

I crossed to open the door to Dykstra, and we sat down together on the bunk. I was irritated to find myself shaking, and more irritated that Dykstra seemed oblivious to it. He was too energized by the meeting with Tanello. He put a finger to his lips, then stood and started moving round the cabin, running his hands along the edge of the built-in furniture and around the portholes.

"You're looking for bugs?" I whispered incredulously. He shushed me again. The search was quickly completed, and he returned to the bunk.

"I already searched my cabin and there was nothing there, but I wanted to make sure. Tanello *has* to be the criminal connection, the one with the organization that helps smuggle the diamonds and dispose of them in the US. He's the link I've been looking for." Dykstra's eyes gleamed in the low light of the cabin.

" You've been looking for *him*? But he's the one who engineered *us* being here. He's been looking for *us*!" I wanted to keep my voice low, but in spite of myself, I heard my tone rise out of control. At least it made Dykstra refocus his attention on me.

"Oh, Sarah, I'm sorry!" He wrapped his arms around me and pulled me to his chest. My cheek was pressed against his shirt and I breathed in his smell, a trace of leather and citrus, warm and sharp at the same time. I heard his heartbeat. "I shouldn't have involved you in this. I've been selfish. I wanted you here, but I didn't think it through. Look, it's not too late, you can leave now—
"

We heard footsteps on the dock at the same moment, and looked up in time to see a pair of sturdy boots walking past the portholes. We both held our breath as they receded, and were rewarded by the change of sound as the steps turned onto the metal gangplank, then muffled noises which might have been voices on the stern deck .

"The missing crewman." Dykstra said. "Sarah, please, if you have any concerns about this, let's make some excuse – a sick aunt or something – and we'll get you off the yacht." But then we heard the screech of steel cable: the gangplank being winched aboard. Too late now to abandon ship, but with Dykstra still holding me, I was feeling calm again. I sat back a little so I could see his face.

"No, it's OK, but what do you think Tanello wants with us? I don't have the sphinx any longer, and you'd think he'd want to keep well clear of an investigative journalist like you if he's involved in crime."

Dykstra frowned."Perhaps he thinks you still have it, or whatever it contains. You told Lelana that the sphinx had been stolen, Lelana told Marco who presumably told Tanello. What if Tanello just doesn't believe it? Or thinks you'd already taken the diamonds out of it?"

"But didn't you think it could be the criminal connection – Tanello's organization – that arranged the break-in at my place? In which case he already has the sphinx and the diamonds. It doesn't make sense." We kept our voices hushed, listening hard for other sounds from above deck. The sudden roar of the ship's engines took us by surprise. They pulsed into life somewhere under our feet, and the floor of the cabin vibrated gently. Through the porthole I saw the distance to the dock increase, and then, as we passed the last lamp on the harbor wall, fade into darkness. We were heading out of the marina towards the open sea.

"What happens now? We should have a plan." I said it as if I knew what I was talking about. As if I had ever been in this situation before. I suppressed a hiccough of hysteria. Dykstra's arm was still firmly around my shoulders. He sighed and hugged me closer.

"It's going to be alright. I think Tanello just wants to know what we know. We convince him we know nothing, he puts us ashore, we say goodbye, and it's all over."

"But . . . . " A question had been jabbing the underside of my consciousness ever since we returned to the *Glissando* after dinner. "Did Marco kill Lelana? He's the police's prime suspect. He's the last one to see her alive, as far as we know. And he takes orders from Tanello. What if Lelana was killed as punishment for losing the sphinx? " I didn't want to put my next thought into words: if Lelana was killed so casually, what were our lives worth?

I think Dykstra was thinking the same thing. "Let me stay here with you tonight. I don't mean sleep with you. Well, I want to, but – this is sounding wrong! I just want to protect you, be here in case something happens." He was stammering, even blushing a little. "I noticed there are no locks on the cabin doors."

I looked over at the door, and immediately saw he was right. "Yes. Stay here. I'd feel safer."

We were in open water now, the yacht riding forward over a gentle swell. The rise and fall was not unpleasant. The engine note had lowered to a steady growl, over which I could hear the slap of water against the hull. I craned over to look up through the porthole at an inky sky pierced with stars. There was no moon, but as we drew further away from the lights on land, the ocean itself glowed with a luminescence that was almost eerie. It was nearly midnight. I suddenly felt exhausted.

"We should try to get some rest. You go ahead and use the bathroom first."

When Dykstra had disappeared into the head, I changed into sweat pants and t-shirt, my usual sleep attire, although I had a much sexier silk slip in my bag. It was difficult to remember my lighthearted mood when I had packed it just this morning, anticipating the fulfillment of my romantic fantasies. Now that I was actually on the point of sharing a bed with Dykstra, romance was not on my mind. Yes, I desperately wanted Dykstra close to me, but not for sex. Earlier, alone in the cabin, I had felt the little sharp-toothed demons that presaged an anxiety attack gnawing at my stomach and pressing down on my lungs. Then, when he held me close, the demons disappeared. He made me feel safe, a sensation I had been searching for most of my life. I could rationalize that this was because I knew he was experienced at moving in and out of dangerous situations, that he knew these people and their world, but it was vaguer and more elemental than that. His arms around me, my head against his chest—it felt like home to me, a home I had never known.

I was mulling over this thought, recapturing the sensation of his body against mine, when he came out of the bathroom. There was a moment of silence, our eyes fixed on each other. I felt he was reading my mind—no, he was *in* my mind, touching me more intimately than a hand could do. Although a moment before I had rejected the idea of sex, I felt a sudden heat throughout my body. I stood and crossed the few feet between us.

"Pieter . . ." We kissed, lips brushing against lips tentatively at first, then more urgently. We stumbled together as the yacht crested a wave. I felt his body straining at mine and his hand on my neck. He pulled his head back a little, and looked at me questioningly.

"I think that's the first time you've used my name."

I laughed weakly, and hid my face in his shirt, the two of us rocking as one with the motion of the sea.

116

"I told you I'm no good at relationships. And my timing sucks too."

He sighed.

"When this is all over, when we get off this damn boat—"

"Yacht," I corrected him teasingly.

"We'll go away somewhere. We'll take the time to get to know each other. I want this to work, Sarah."

Me too, I thought as we kissed again, now with more restraint, both of us knowing we would not make love this night, that we would save the ultimate act of intimacy for another place and time.

***

I woke abruptly. It took some seconds to orient myself. I had not meant to fall asleep. I was lying between the bulkhead and Dykstra's body. A low light from the bathroom illuminated the cabin. Something had woken me, but I didn't know what. Then I heard a soft movement in the passageway outside. Dykstra squeezed my hand. He was awake too. I could see his face just inches from mine, eyes alert. Then, with surprising speed, he spun away and off the bunk. He grabbed the cabin door handle as the door began to open inward, and stood there like a bulwark against whoever was trying to enter.

"Pieter! I was hoping I might find you two together." Tanello sounded friendly, as if he had just bumped into us at the neighborhood coffee shop. "I thought this might be a good time to have a talk, while everything's quiet."

Tanello slid quickly past Dykstra, who was a moment too late in his attempt to shut the door. He had little choice but to return to my side. He reached down for my hand again, and I stood up, pressing close to his shoulder. I took a quick glimpse at my watch: two-twenty a.m. We must be well south of Hilton Head by now and out of coastal waters. Tanello was still dressed in his chinos and Hawaiian shirt, looking as unruffled as he had earlier. There was no seating in the cabin other than the bunk, so he stood leaning casually against the wall looking at us speculatively.

I had the urge to scream at him to get the hell out of my room. How could he assume it was permissible to just amble in for a chat in the early hours of the morning? But I swiftly remembered the real dynamic behind his amiable demeanor. He held all the cards. We were on his boat, perhaps by now outside of US waters. He could do what he damn well liked. I bit my lip in frustration mixed with dread.

Dykstra's silence had a different quality. I could sense him calculating options that might shift the power balance in the room. After a second or two, Tanello shrugged, smirking a little, as if to say *OK, you win this round, as if I cared.*

"Why don't we move up to the day cabin, where we can all be more comfortable?"

"I don't think so. It's really late, and Sarah's tired. The conversation can surely wait until the morning, when we're all rested." I admired the way Dykstra kept his voice level, but communicated an iron resolve.

"Oh—" As if suddenly reminded of something, Tanello turned to open the cabin door wider."Marco, could you help me escort them upstairs?"

Before he had finished speaking, Marco was inside. I gasped when I saw the gun in his fist.

"No, Marco, put that away. I don't want bullet holes in the hull." Tanello chuckled."Anyway, I'm sure it's not necessary. Pieter and Sarah will agree to come with us now."

"Mr. Tanello, what is it you want? Just tell us. If we can help you, we will. There's no need for threats." Dykstra's voice remained as even as Tanello's.

"Lou, please, just call me Lou. And I completely agree. No need for threats. So, shall we?" He walked past Marco and

118

stood smiling back at us from the passageway. Marco, who had obediently tucked his gun back into the waistband of his pants, took a step forward as if to grab hold of us, but Dykstra put up a warning hand, and, bowing to the inevitable, we stood and followed Tanello out of the cabin and up the stairway to the main deck.

The blinds in the day cabin had been pulled tightly down, even over the double glass doors that led out to the stern deck. The champagne bucket, glasses and tulips had been removed. The only items on the low glass coffee table now were a pack of Gitanes cigarettes in their iconic blue wrapping and a heavy-looking gold table lighter, though I could see no ashtray. Marco took up his position by the doors, arms crossed, face blank. I suddenly remembered that Marco was supposed to be our captain. The question of who was now steering the yacht preoccupied me briefly until Tanello walked over to a wall-mounted phone.

"Mel? You can reduce speed now. …. Yes, just enough power to keep us steady. Thanks."

Instantly, the engine noise lessened, and the motion of the yacht changed from a consistent up-and-down forward movement over the waves, to a gentler sway as we rocked between them.

"Sit, please." Tanello indicated the sofa across the table from where he had placed himself. We sat. Dykstra held my hand in both of his. I had a ridiculous fleeting image of him as the young suitor seeking permission to marry me from my father, the figure now leaning earnestly towards us. I gave my head a quick shake to dispel the distraction, and tried to concentrate on Tanello's words.

"Sarah, I'm really puzzled about your role in all this. You have so much to lose! Why get involved?"

It was weird how these questions echoed the ones I had asked myself repeatedly, but I kept control of my expression and answered coolly.

119

"Role in what, exactly? I don't understand. I met Pieter recently in London. Then he visited me in Atlanta, and invited me to go sailing with him and his friends, Arun and Paul. I thought the yacht was theirs. "

"Come on! I know you know more than that, Sarah, please don't insult my intelligence. Pieter, you're too much of a gentleman to let a lady try to shield you. Let's just be honest with each other."

"Lou, why don't you start – with the honesty, I mean? How did you meet Arun and Paul, and what do you know about Lelana? " Dykstra had switched into reporter mode. I almost expected him to whip out a notebook and pencil.

Tanello laughed pleasantly. "Pieter, so many questions! Let's start with the fact that I know you were using poor Lelana, and I know what you were using her for." He switched his gaze to look appraisingly at me."Now I wonder if Sarah knew about that?"

I opened my mouth to speak but Dykstra's quick squeeze of my hand stopped me.

"Lelana was helping me with a story, a story my agency published last May about Middle-Eastern rulers and how they hide their personal wealth. We became lovers. And, yes, Sarah knows all about it."

"I'm afraid he's lying to you, Sarah." Tanello smiled kindly at me. "Pieter is after much more than a story, aren't you, Pieter? Lelana was so gullible, so ready to believe you. You were her knight in shining armor, rescuing her from the nasty ogre her father had promised her to. Yes, I know about that too. And what did you tell Sarah? What ogre are you rescuing her from?"

His false front of friendliness was grating badly on my nerves. It took all my training to keep my posture relaxed and my face bland. I let Dykstra respond.

"Look, Lou. I can see what you're trying to do: drive a wedge between Sarah and me. Undermine her trust in me so she'll tell you what you want to know. But she doesn't know anything! So it's a wasted effort. Just ask me the questions. I'm not sure I know anything either, but let's stop playing games."

For the briefest moments, Tanello's veneer of *bonhomie* cracked, and his lips narrowed into a thin line. I didn't like the dead look in his eyes as they flicked between us. Then he resumed his mask and leaned back, gazing regretfully up at the ceiling.

"Games ...... I wish this *was* all just a game, but it's not. There's an enormous amount of money at stake, and you know that, Pieter. So," He sat back up, clapping his hands together, miming the jovial businessman ready to get down to business. "Here's what we'll do. Marco will take Pieter up to the crew's quarters while I interview Sarah here."

Almost before he had finished speaking, Dykstra lunged across the table, his hands stretched towards Tanello's neck. But Marco arrested his forward movement, grabbing Dykstra's shoulders with both hands and hauling him sideways over the table and onto his back on the floor. He then pinned him down by kneeling across his neck and chest. I was on my feet, but before I could do anything to intervene – what, I had no idea - Tanello had miraculously transported himself to my side and had my arm, the one with the bullet wound, twisted up behind my back. His other arm was across my throat, forcing my whole body back against his. I realized the loose Hawaiian shirt hid a physique that was anything but average. It felt as if I was backed up against a brick wall. Meanwhile Dykstra's face was turning a deep red, as Marco's bulk weighed down on him. The tussle was over in less than ten seconds.

"Be good." Tanello hissed in my ear. I tried to wrench my head away from his mouth, but his grip tightened and the pain across my throat and in my arm immobilized me. "Marco, give me one of those."

Marco had flipped Dykstra onto his stomach as if he weighed no more than a child, and linked his wrists behind him with what looked like the plastic tie for a garbage bag. Marco tossed another plastic tie across the coffee table. Tanello reached for it, pushing me down into a kneeling position in the process. He pulled my arms behind me and cinched the tie tight enough to cut into my wrists before throwing me back onto the sofa. I fought for breath, my mouth opening and closing like a fish.

He leaned over me, his face six inches above mine, but he addressed Dykstra.

"Pieter, I want you to go with Marco. The sooner you tell him what I want to know, the sooner you can come back here to Sarah. I want you to be thinking about her, about how I'll get her to talk to me." He spun around and looked at Dykstra with narrowed eyes. "You say she doesn't know anything. I don't believe you. She'll talk; it's just a matter of time. The question is who talks first: you or her."

Dykstra's voice was a harsh croak. "Don't hurt her. I've said I'll answer your questions."

"I know you will, Pieter. Sarah's just my insurance—my way of making sure your answers are truthful."

Dykstra tried to say something else, but Marco had him on his feet, one hand pushing him from behind, the other across his throat. Their bodies close, in an ungainly slow dance, Marco maneuvered him through the doors to the stern deck. Through the throb of pain in my wrists and throat, I heard their stumbling progress around the side deck towards the bow. I struggled into an approximation of a sitting position, still panting, and glared across to where Tanello had resumed his seat, looking as unruffled as before.

"Oh dear, I thought it might come to this." He scooped up the cigarettes and lighter, and made an elaborate show of opening the pack, selecting one, and igniting it with the lighter. He inhaled deeply, making the tip of the cigarette glow orange like a coal. Then he burst out in a paroxysm of coughing mixed with laughter. When he had recovered, he looked thoughtfully at the cigarette before raising his eyes to mine.

"You see, Sarah, I don't actually smoke. This one's for you."

Chapter 13

When I came to consciousness, the first sensation was thirst. My tongue was stuck to the roof of my mouth. I prised it loose and ran it laboriously over my teeth. All present and correct, as far as I could remember, which wasn't far. Was I blind? Everything was dark. Experimentally, I cracked open one lid. An explosion of light and memory. My whole body burned with pain. I sank back below consciousness to regroup.

When I awoke again, I fought through the universal pain to take stock of the specifics: a clammy cold feeling around my bottom half. I had wet myself! The humiliation catapulted me back to childhood. The acrid smell of fresh urine mixed with the dusty-musty-sweaty smell of bedding gone too long unwashed. And fear. The smell of fear. I would be punished for soiling myself, and for soiling the bed, no matter how dirty the sheets already were. Tears, and memories of tears shed a lifetime ago, finally unglued my eyes.

I was lying on my side on the pale leather sofa, facing into the room, knees drawn up in a fetal position, arms still pinioned behind my back. My face was level with the coffee table. Across the glassy expanse, I saw two dark blobs. It took me a moment to work out they were knees clad in denim, and, between them, a shining globe that resolved itself into Marco's face, the rest of his body foreshortened by the angle of my view. Light bounced off his shaved skull, like a Renaissance painting of an obscure saint. Marco, patron saint of lost statues, lost causes, lost reason.

Time passed. Jagged pieces fell into place. I remembered Tanello's questions and my answers, repeated into an infinity of images, as if captured between reflecting mirrors, punctuated by pain.

"Where's the sphinx?"

"Don't know."

Tanello extinguishing a cigarette on my upper arm, due north of the still-raw bullet scar.

"Did you remove the diamonds?"

"No."

Another wrong answer, another cigarette burn pressed to my flesh.

"Where are the diamonds?"

"Don't know."

East, west, south. The entire compass rose appeared on my bicep, and still I could not seem to get the answers right. At some point, Tanello appeared to lose interest in my responses, asking the questions by rote, a mantra to justify the continuing torture. He had flipped me on my stomach by then, and had ripped down my sweat pants and underwear. My buttocks clenched against the sexual assault I was sure would come. But Tanello, his voice as even as my dentist's asking me to open wider, satisfied himself with more cigarette burns. The scent of a Parisian café mingled with the aroma of burgers on the grill. I gagged and buried my face in the leather to escape. The reduced air supply drove me to the edge of blackness but not quite into it.

In my delirium, I heard my father's hillbilly accent.

"C'mon, Sally Ann, I'm your daddy. Stop crying, or I'll give you something to cry about!"

"Don't hurt me, Daddy, please ..... "

After that, reality and memory drowned in the same dark pool.

***

I heard the door glide open between the day cabin and the saloon. I forced my eyes open and saw Marco in the same position as before across the other side of the table. I craned my head painfully upwards to see who was entering. Ingrid stood braced in the opening. She was wearing a man's shirt and no shoes. Her fleshless thighs were shaking, and her eyes skittered across from Marco to me. Even in my semi-lucid state, I could tell she was on drugs.

"Where is he? I gotta …. What's with her? Listen, he said he'd take care of … is she sick or what?"

"He's busy. Go back to bed."

I realized then I had never heard Marco speak. I now understood why: his voice was high, unnaturally high for a man of his size. He tried to disguise it by barely opening his mouth, but the effect was to make him sound even more babyish, a distinct disadvantage for a thug.

"Yeah, sure, when I get what I need. Where is he?" She repeated, losing interest in me. She was preoccupied with her own plight, bending forward, arms held tight across her stomach.

Tanello appeared quietly at the double doors from the stern deck. He advanced calmly towards Ingrid and slapped her face hard, left, right, with his open hand. She staggered, and her mouth fell open, but she managed to hold herself upright against the door frame. Except for the sharp crack of hand against cheek, the cabin was silent. Marco had not moved a muscle; Ingrid gaped at Tanello but said nothing. After a second, Tanello extracted a small packet from his shirt pocket and stuffed it into Ingrid's open mouth. She dropped her gaze. Turning, she palmed the packet and

126

scuttled towards the bow and the dubious safety of the master stateroom.

Tanello dismissed Marco with a gesture, then, when Marco had closed the doors to the deck behind him, he turned to me.

"So, Sarah, it seems you were telling the truth after all. You really don't know anything." He pursed his lips and shook his head, miming – what? Pity? Regret? I knew better than to try and interpret Tanello's mild-mannered comments. The man was a sadist, cold as ice and lethal as poison. I kept my mouth shut, and concentrated hard. If I was going to make it out of this situation, I could not afford to lose my grip on reality and slip into some ugly backwater of childhood memory. Nor could I let anxiety steal my breath away. Unconsciousness had been my sanctuary earlier; now I had to stay alert.

Tanello fixed me with his colorless eyes. "Pieter talked. He told me everything. I must say I'm surprised. Lelana was young and inexperienced. Not a shock that Pieter could take advantage of her. But you! I find it hard to believe you didn't see through him. How could you think he didn't know what was in the sphinx? It was so obvious! He used you, Sarah. You were his mule. He knew where Lelana had hidden the diamonds, and he transferred them to you right under her nose. He isn't after a story. He already had the story; it was published months ago. He's after the diamonds."

No, I refused to believe him. If I'd had my hands free, I would have pressed them to my ears to keep out the soft-spoken slander Tanello was feeding me. Pieter was a good man. He must be, otherwise why would I have felt that instinctive trust when he held me in his arms? I had spent years building a fortress around myself; it could not be possible that the first person to penetrate it was a traitor. .....Could it?

I was still lying on my side on the sofa, my wounded arm uppermost. I had managed to drag my pants up over the burns on my buttocks. Now, I slowly pulled myself up to a seated position. Without use of arms and hands, it required all my core muscle strength. The moment I achieved vertical and sank back against the sofa cushions, thunderbolts of pain shot up from my rear-end through my spine, bouncing against the interior of my skull. I fought the urge to close my eyes, and willed myself to maintain Tanello's gaze. He had been enjoying watching my struggle to sit up, and the obvious pain it caused me.

"But Pieter doesn't have the diamonds." I croaked.

"No," Tanello conceded. "That's the missing piece. His partner, the burglar who broke into your house to retrieve the sphinx, after you so helpfully brought it into the States, seems to have disappeared. Maybe the partner has betrayed Pieter, just like Pieter betrayed Lelana and you, or maybe he's just lying low, waiting for the dust to settle before disposing of the stones and splitting the proceeds with Pieter."

"Pieter doesn't know where the diamonds are."   Again, I kept my voice neutral, focusing on facts. For the moment, I pushed aside any interpretation of motives, especially Dykstra's motives. "So why not let us go?"

"*Because they're my diamonds!*"   The sudden change of pitch took me by surprise. Perhaps it surprised Tanello too, because he took a few seconds to smooth down his shirt and examine his nails before continuing.

"I've spent a lot of time and money cultivating these Arab playboys. It's a serious investment. I would think you could understand that, Sarah. You know how business works. It's all about service these days. I—that is, my organization – provides a service. We have to convince our customers our service is reliable and better than anyone else's. Once we've won their trust, well, …. I can't let Pieter ruin all that, can I?"

And me? That should have been my next question. If Tanello now understood that I had no idea where the diamonds were, why couldn't he let *me* go? But instead, my brain circled around the word 'betrayal': according to Tanello, Pieter wasn't after a story, he was after the diamonds. It was certainly possible he knew they were in the sphinx when he gave it to me in London. He knew my Atlanta address. He could have arranged the break-in, and then, pretending to follow Lelana, have come to the US to retrieve and dispose of the jewels. What I had imagined as the start of a love affair was possibly no more than a convenient transaction to him. Forty-year old unattached woman risks her reputation and security to transport illicit goods across international boundaries, lies to the police and undergoes torture, all to help a greedy journalist cash in on a smuggling ring. Laughable, really, if it wasn't so humiliating. The humiliation stung almost as deeply as the cigarette burns.

***

It would start to get light soon. The boat was still drifting at minimum speed. I assumed Dykstra was now under Marco's guard in the forward crew quarters. I wondered whether Tanello had used cigarettes on him too, but I thought it more likely he had let Marco employ more brutal tactics. Tanello, though surprisingly muscular, was not as big as Dykstra, and I didn't think he would risk getting in too close. Also, I had observed that he got a perverted pleasure from torturing me, a woman. There wouldn't be the same satisfaction from hurting a man. My stomach lurched when I thought about the damage Marco might have inflicted with those huge fists. Was Dykstra even still alive? If he had lied to me as Tanello suggested, I shouldn't care. Yet I still recalled the sensation of safety when he held me in his arms the night before, and the way we had kissed. I alternated between the memory of that instinctual trust, and what my early experience had taught me: the very people who were supposed to care about me would hurt and abandon me.

129

More practically, I also thought about what would happen when Arun and Paul staggered above decks, nursing their hangovers, searching blearily for coffee, and expecting to see the emerald slopes and aquamarine waters of Gran Bahama to the south. I was sure that the boys, although hardly innocent, were Tanello's dupes too. To them he was a "fixer," someone who took care of the problems of the super-rich. They would not have inquired too deeply into his methods. However, they might panic if forced to confront them. It was one thing for a drugged-out call girl to occupy the master suite. It would be quite another to find the beaten bodies of a respected journalist – their own drinking buddy – and his lady friend decorating the day cabin. My best guess was that Tanello would try to dispose of us before dawn. Arun and Paul would probably swallow any story he fed them later about an emergency call and an early departure. I had to figure out a way to free myself, then find a place to hide until we were in port and I could escape. That was the movie script where anything was possible with special effects and stunt doubles; this unfortunately was real life.

Minutes crawled by. Tanello was busy with his smartphone, flipping through apps silently, not even looking at me now. I was deciding whether to ask for water - I was desperately thirsty, but didn't want to show Tanello any weakness – when the onboard telephone buzzed. Tanello reached up and unhooked it from the wall. He listened briefly, grunted a few affirmatives, and hung up. At last, he looked over at me coldly, but said nothing. I was just an inconvenience to him now: I didn't know where the diamonds were, and I couldn't be allowed to live.

No doubt summoned by Tanello during the onboard call, Marco entered from the stern deck, thrusting Dykstra in front of him. I barely recognized him. His face was bloodied, and both eyes were swollen to mere cracks in the bruised and puffy skin. His shirt was torn open, revealing scarlet welts across his chest and throat. His legs didn't work properly; forward motion was achieved only by Marco's knee pushing against the backs of his thighs. His arms were still tied behind him.

It suddenly didn't matter what Tanello said: I believed in Dykstra. Involuntarily, I tried to rise and stretch out my arms towards him, forgetting in my shock that my arms were restrained too. I fell awkwardly off the sofa, ending up on my knees at Dykstra's feet. I doubted that he could see anything, but he turned his head to the noise.

"Pieter! It's me, Sarah. I'm here!"

He aimed his poor battered face down toward my voice.

"Sarah ...." His voice cracked, and he slumped face down. He would have fallen on top of me, but for Marco savagely jerking him upright and pushing him onto the banquette opposite. I knee-walked over to him, expecting Marco or Tanello to grab me and pull me away, but they didn't.

"It's O.K. I'm here. We're alive. It's going to be all right."

Tanello barked out a derisive laugh. It *was* one of the stupider things I've said in my life, but I wanted to comfort him anyway I could. I could feel fresh blood dripping down where I had reopened the ligature wounds on my wrists. I remembered the first night we met. My blood had dripped on the floor then too. Was my bloodshed to be the parentheses of our relationship? I lay my head gently down on the pale leather next to his, my mouth against his ear. He struggled to pull his face out of the cushions.

"Sarah, I'm so sorry ..."

"Shhhh, it's all right ..." We whispered to each other like the lovers we had planned to be. I was pierced with regret that we had never made love, and now never would.

There was movement at the sliding doors to the stern deck, but I kept my eyes fixed on Dykstra's face just inches from mine.

A voice I didn't recognize spoke.

"You ready to crank up the engines? If we want to get there before noon, we should put some speed on."

"Hey, Mel!" Tanello had resumed his so-happy-to-meet-you tone. "Yeah, full steam ahead! Get back up on the bridge. Don't worry about all this. Marco'll clean it up."

I heard the doors close, and a tense silence descended on the day cabin. Then the engines revved up and the yacht pulsed forward at speed, knocking me to the deck. It must have surprised Tanello and Marco too, because when I scrambled around to see what was happening, Tanello was sideways on the opposite sofa, and Marco was scrabbling to hold on to an upright next to the door.

"Sonofabitch!" I took a bitter joy in seeing Tanello's equilibrium upset. He steadied himself, and as soon as the yacht's motion regained a rhythm, rose to his feet.

"Take care of them. No guns. Don't want to wake the Arabs. Just …" He made a gesture towards the stern, then rolled his shoulders to release tension. "I'm tired. It's been a long night."

Without sparing another glance at Dykstra and me, he opened the door to the saloon and headed forward to his master stateroom.

My mind raced feverishly between one impossible option and the next. Was there anything I could use as a weapon? Something sharp I could stick in Marco's eye? I had seen this in a movie where the kidnapped star had overcome her much bigger captor. But even if there was a weapon, my hands were tied. Disabled like this, could I manage a well-aimed kick to Marco's groin? And if by some miracle I could push Marco off-balance, could I hope that Dykstra had enough strength left to back me up? This was another movie fantasy: his hands were tied too, and I didn't think he was even conscious.

But Marco was taking no chances. Perhaps he had seen the same films I had. He spoke in his little girl voice.

132

"You, move over here to the other sofa." He stayed by the doors to the deck until I complied. Then he opened the doors and went back over to where Dykstra was lying. So he was going to throw Dykstra overboard first, then come back for me. A gust of sea air rushed into the day cabin. It smelled clean and sweet. I blinked back tears of self pity. Just to breathe fresh air invoked the blessings of a normal life, blessings I had taken for granted only hours earlier. I strained to see outside. A faint salmon pink line separated sea from sky. The sun would be up soon to turn the charcoal gray to blue, but I wouldn't be alive to see that daily miracle.

Marco dragged Dykstra's inert body through the door and angled for the rail. Suddenly a dark shadow fell on top of Marco with a thud, collapsing him down onto Dykstra, forming a small mountain of bodies on the deck. There was a brief inchoate struggle; I heard a gurgling sound, then silence. I sat motionless, not breathing, not yet daring to interpret this turn of events. The top part of the mountain of bodies separated and rose, resolving itself into the shape of a man.

"C'mon, let's get out of here." I recognized his voice. It was the man called Mel, who had discomfited Tanello by coming down in person from the bridge to get instructions. He was fortyish, clean shaven and with hair cut military-short. I must have been gaping like an idiot because he came forward into the lighted day cabin and pulled me up by my arm. I let out a cry of pain. He spun me round and quickly freed the plastic ligature around my wrists.

"Quiet! Get moving. I'll need your help with him." He handed me the Swiss army knife he had used to cut the plastic tie, and indicated the tangle of bodies by the rail. I approached gingerly, half-expecting Marco to rise up with a roar and grab me, but when I managed after a struggle to separate his considerable weight from Dykstra's body, the light that seeped out of the cabin

133

revealed bulbous staring eyes and a thin red line deeply incised into his throat. He was definitely dead. With some difficulty, I edged Dykstra into a sitting position and cut through his restraints. He moaned but didn't open his eyes. I sat close, stroking his hands and cheeks, trying to rouse him to consciousness.

Our rescuer was busy at a console panel at the stern. He was setting switches that appeared to control the mechanism which suspended the yacht's inflatable tender out over the stern. A whirring noise discernable over the sound of the yacht's engines announced the descent of the inflatable towards the water. It halted just below the level of the railing that bordered the deck, and hung there swaying. 1 looked around, anxious that at the last moment someone would arrive on the stern deck to frustrate our escape.

Mel bent over me, keeping his voice low. "This is going to be tricky. The yacht's supposed to be stopped when the tender's lowered. We'll get him in, then you follow, and I'll jump for it as soon as I've released the ropes. Let's hope she doesn't capsize."

Between us, we pulled and pushed Dykstra to the stern rail. The bottom of the inflatable was barely visible about three feet below us. Even if we could get Dykstra's inert body over the rail, I was afraid he would break a limb in the fall. As I hesitated, Mel took charge, and, with no apparent effort, tipped Dykstra inelegantly over into the inflatable. I think his lack of consciousness helped him fall loosely, without damage. Mel gestured for me to follow, and before he could assist me, I climbed over and jumped down next to Dykstra. I crouched over him, feeling the shaking of the fragile bottom of the dinghy through my feet.

"Brace yourselves." Sitting with his feet dangling outside the stern rail, Mel leaned back to work the controls, then, just as the ropes that secured the boat to the derricks released, he flung himself forward. The dinghy crashed down onto the water, rocking dangerously, and Mel fell onto all fours almost on top of me. I scrambled for a handhold, blinded by spray. With my other hand I groped for Dykstra's arm, terrified he might roll out into the ocean just at the moment we made our getaway.

"Who are you?" The shock of cold water had revived Dykstra. He was lying in the bottom of the boat, legs splayed out in front of him, peering through his swollen eyelids at our rescuer.

"Special Agent Mel Harbrough, FBI. And this is the most screwed-up under-cover op I've ever been involved in."

Chapter 14

The inflatable dinghy dropped back behind the *Glissando* surprisingly quickly. One minute we were careening wildly in the yacht's wake; the next we were bobbing gently up and down. The sound of the larger boat's engines faded away in the distance, and its lights – the bright white pinpoint of the stern light and the muted yellow glow that escaped from the day cabin – receded into the pre-dawn darkness. It occurred to me that the *Glissando* was a ghost ship: no one at the helm, and its passengers either dead – the thin red line incised into Marco's throat flashed through my mind – or sleeping. I did not spend long pondering their fate before my own physical predicament brought me back to my present situation in the dinghy.

My sweatpants between my thighs had been damp with urine before the rescue. What had plunged me into a nightmare of half-remembered childhood trauma when I was still in the clutches of my tormentor now seemed inconsequential. The rest of me was soaked too now, caught by the wave that nearly swamped the inflatable when it fell into the sea. The burns on my upper arm and buttocks had dulled to a constant nagging, which only burst into a flame of pain when I moved too quickly, pressing salt-water-soaked fabric against them. I gripped the guide rope that circled the boat, and gingerly tried to find an angle where I was not putting pressure on the burns on my buttocks. I allowed my mind to contemplate what had happened over the last few hours. I was like a child peeping through her fingers at a horror movie, looking at a little slice of the terror before running back to the safety of the fact of my survival. I was alive. Against all the odds, I had been rescued. And gradually a weird kind of energy welled up in me. I was alive!

Mel Harbrough was rooting around in the pouches that lined the inside of the inflatable. He pulled out two thermal blankets, one side a foil-like surface, the other red fleece.

"Wrap those around yourselves, foil side out." He said gruffly, and continued his search for supplies.

Gritting my teeth against the pain, I shuffled sideways to tuck one blanket around Dykstra. He was semi-conscious, and obviously in a lot of pain. His breathing was uneven, and he had a glazed look that worried me. I covered myself with the other blanket. It was only when I was under its protection that I realized how cold I was. I started shivering. And then I found myself crying, great gulping sobs I tried hard to suppress. Having basically kept it together until now, I could not understand why I was experiencing this loss of control. Delayed shock, I guessed. Probably the natural side effect of a near-collision with death.

"Here." Harbrough thrust a plastic bottle of water at me, ignoring my tears. "You should get him to drink some too." He indicated Dykstra with a jerk of his head. "And see what's in here." He pushed across a box with a red cross marked on its lid, then turned his back on us to fiddle with the outboard motor. His tone discouraged questions, even if I had wanted conversation. The need for action, if only to unscrew the bottle top and hold it to Dykstra's lips, calmed me somewhat. I found a packet of antiseptic swabs in the first aid kit, and opened it with difficulty. Cleaning the blood off Dykstra's face made it look even worse. I used some butterfly band aids to pull together the edges of the cuts around his eyes. I was surprised that I was able to do all this with a modicum of efficiency, in fact that I was able to do it at all. I had never been drawn to nursing, and had had no opportunity to practice these kinds of skills. I guess it was a way of coping with shock: concentrate on the practical.

The outboard burst into life, and the bow where Dykstra and I were half-sitting, half-lying tilted up abruptly, as the little boat surged forward and made a steep turn away from the salmon pink eastern horizon. I grabbed the guideline with one hand and Dykstra's shirt with the other to prevent us sliding towards the stern. The hard irregular slaps onto the water's surface made further first aid impossible. The three of us crouched in our own cones of silence, me and Dykstra huddled in the bow facing Harbrough at the tiller in the stern.

I turned to take stock of Dykstra. I thought the warmth of the blanket and a few sips of water had steadied him, but he continued to stare fixedly towards the horizon beyond Harbrough's head. At least, he was alive. I mentally relived our exchange the night before in my cabin. The certainty that we would be lovers – that we already *were* lovers, bound by an emotional connection every bit as real as the physical – surged through me like a kind of euphoria, and I started weeping again. I felt as tossed about by my emotions as the inflatable on the ocean. I beamed at Dykstra through my tears, trying to communicate my elation at our mutual survival, and was rewarded by a weak but convincing smile in response. I held his eyes for a long moment, willing him to be alright, not damaged in any profound way by the horrors he had experienced, to be still the Dykstra who had held me as I'd always wanted to be held and kissed me as I had never been kissed before.

***

Time passed, but I had no sense of how much. We could have been travelling westwards for ten minutes or an hour. The band of lighter sky behind Harbrough's head had widened and turned amber at its upper edge. I could see our rescuer's face more clearly now. He had a strong jaw which he held clenched as if biting down on anger or irritation. He wore a black turtleneck sweater under a light-colored rain jacket, dark jeans and sneakers. He scanned the horizon ahead with narrowed eyes, and I got the sense he was avoiding looking directly at us.

"Where are we?" I shouted to be heard over the racket of the outboard motor.

"Less than five miles off St Augustine," Harbrough replied shortly, still not meeting my eye. I knew St Augustine was south of the Florida-Georgia border, probably less than a hundred miles south of Hilton Head. I craned to look over my shoulder in case I could see any lights on land, but there was nothing, just darkness.

"How long until we get there?"

Harbrough shrugged. "Less than an hour. Maybe."

"What's going to happen to the *Glissando* going full speed ahead with no one steering?" His taciturnity was a challenge to me. I was determined to keep asking questions until he opened up.

"The Coast Guard'll board it and take control. There's been a ship shadowing the *Glissando* since we left port."

I slowly took this in. My mind was working at a snail's pace. Then the pieces fell into place.

"The Coast Guard's been following us? All the time Tanello was—and Marco was torturing Pieter? And they—you—did nothing?" I was nearly shrieking now, incoherent with fury.

"What the hell—?" Dykstra was trying to struggle up from where he had been propped against the side of the dinghy, shifting in and out of awareness.

"Get down, both of you, and shut up." The FBI agent looked at us finally, his face grim and mouth set in an angry line. "We spent three painstaking, dangerous months trying to get close to Tanello and his organization. I had to do things . . . difficult, disgusting things, just to get inside. And now that's all wasted. I had to kill a man tonight to save your sorry hides. And doing that, I blew the lid off the under-cover operation. It's ruined. All that effort down the drain." Now he had started talking, he was not going to stop. "The Coast Guard will find nothing – no black market diamonds, no drugs. Just a dead thug—the one *I* killed - and a doped-up call girl. Oh, and two very well-connected young foreigners who'll be screaming about diplomatic immunity, and getting the State Department to hush it all up. Tanello will walk away, and we'll be back to zero. You're angry? Imagine how I feel." He glared at us, then made a disgusted sound and resumed scanning the sea ahead.

"But can't we testify against him? I mean Pieter and me? What he and Marco did was criminal assault at least."

Harbrough barked out a short laugh.

"That's not how it works, lady. You have no witnesses, and Tanello can afford the best lawyers. They'll have you tied up in knots, *if* you could ever find a prosecutor who'd pursue a case based on conduct on the high seas."

Dykstra had found strength from somewhere. Wincing with pain, he leaned forward to focus.

"But you are a witness. You know what happened."

"Are you listening to me? It's outside US jurisdiction. International waters. There will be no prosecution."

I felt shell-shocked by the realization that during the entire horrible ordeal, help had been at hand and withheld. My rage ebbed as fast as it had flowed, replaced by a dreary feeling of frustration. Tanello had beaten all of us. Dykstra sank back again, drained by the effort of the exchange with Harbrough. I edged closer to him and found his hand under the blanket. I wanted to ask him what Marco and Tanello had done to him, but I was afraid to hear his answer. He seemed diminished, not the confident journalist on the scent of a story who had swept my cabin for bugs the night before.

140

"Pieter, is there anything I can do to make you more comfortable? I cleaned up what I could see ….."

He turned his battered face away. "Marco used electric shock … on my spine." He faced me then, his eyes wide and his mouth quivering in fear. "I can't move my legs! I think I'm … paralyzed."

Dear God, no. What should I do? What should I say?

"Can you feel them?" I reached under the blanket below his knee and squeezed his calf.

"Yes, yes, I can feel that. It's just they're so weak. It's hard to move them, and I don't think I can stand up." I could hear the panic in his voice.

"Well, don't try and stand up here. Flex your feet, wiggle your toes, if you can. Perhaps it's just temporary." I was reluctant to do it, given the hostility he had shown to us, but Harbrough was my only resource. I shouted over the outboard engine's racket. "Agent Harbrough, what do you know about electric shocks to the spine? That's what Marco did to Pieter, and his legs won't work. Will it wear off?"

Harbrough shrugged. I could have cheerfully killed him.

"Look, land." He pointed over our shoulders and we turned to see faintly glowing in a line on the horizon what must have been the lights of St. Augustine or Jacksonville, some Atlantic coast community slowly waking to the new day, oblivious to criminals, torture, smuggling – everything we had been plunged into in the last half dozen hours. We all three looked landward like pilgrims sighting America for the first time. We could even see the outline of the land, black against a slightly paler sky. After a long pause, Harbrough answered my question. "Yes, it wears off. There may be after-effects, weakness that comes and goes, but he'll walk again, he's not paralyzed. Ah, at last ….." And then he raised his cell phone to his ear, and muttered into it, turning away so that we couldn't hear him.

141

"See? You'll be OK."

"And you, Sarah? Are you OK? What did he do to you?"

"I'm OK, Pieter. I'm tough!" I made a fist and parodied a little punch to his jaw. He smiled at me then, a mere shadow of the boyish grin that won me over in the hotel restaurant a millenium ago, but still enough to lift my heart. I really did feel tough, too. Maybe just the illusion granted by survival against the odds, a lucky outcome, no thanks to me, but still, what does not kill us makes us strong. I shifted my position to look hopefully toward the approaching Florida coast, Dykstra's hand in mine under the thermal blankets.

Gradually, the features of the coast became clear. We were approaching a beach community: pleasant homes, not mansions, set back from the sand behind scrubby lawns and low bushes. A very few early joggers were out, some with dogs, enjoying the cool dawn air. We were aimed towards a huddle at the water's edge, maybe four men, out of place in their dark business suits. I saw a white van, perhaps an ambulance, pulled up behind this group at the crest of the beach, two people lounging against the vehicle. We were in the surf now, and Harbrough cut back the outboard motor. I expected someone – Harbrough or one of the group on the beach – to shout out, but there was an awkward silence as we drifted in to shore. Finally, one of the group detached himself, and, with a look of disgust on his face, tiptoed into the water to grab the front of the inflatable. As if waiting for that sign, Harbrough jumped out and helped drag the boat onto the beach.

Moment of truth. I stood up and looked down at Dykstra, extending my hand. Nervously scrabbling at the rope that was strung around the upper edge of the boat, he worked himself up to kneeling, then standing. With grins as wide as our faces, we assisted each other over the edge of the inflatable into a foot or so of water. We waded ashore to the serious-looking group, now including Harbrough, gathered at the water's edge.

There was a strange moment of disconnect as we came face to face with the five men ranged in front of us. Dykstra and I were euphoric with our intact survival: Dykstra was able to walk, our wounds would heal, above all, we were alive. Yet the expressions the men wore were grim. Harbrough was looking out to the horizon as if he wanted to be back at sea. The agent – I guessed these were all Harbrough's FBI colleagues – who helped pull us ashore, was looking miserably down at his soaking wet pants legs and shoes. The others stared stonily at us. The silence was broken when the two paramedics ambled down from the vehicle parked on the upper edge of the beach.

"Who needs attention here?"

I gestured towards Dykstra. "I've cleaned up his face but there are other wounds …."

One of the paramedics led Dykstra up the beach.

"What about you, darlin'?"

"Burns on my arm and buttocks. My wrists are a bit cut up." I extended my arms to show him. "But it's him I'm worried about," looking up the incline of the beach to where Dykstra was talking to the first paramedic.

"OK, come with me."

I obediently followed the paramedic up the sand to the ambulance, leaving the other men mumbling together behind me. In the privacy of the vehicle, the paramedic applied antiseptic ointment and taped gauze pads to the burns on my upper arm and buttocks, and the cuts on my wrist. It took no more than five minutes. Just as we were finishing up, the other paramedic swung up into the back of the ambulance.

"Is he OK? My friend? He was cut up pretty bad and electrocuted—"

"Yeah, well, the Fibbies are taking care of him. He'll be OK." He seemed embarrassed, shifting his weight around and avoiding my eye.

"What do you mean?" I thrust past him and jumped down from the back of the vehicle. The beach was empty now. I looked around frantically. Where were the men in suits? Where was Dykstra? I turned back to the paramedics, and caught sight of a car door opening out of the corner of my eye. Several yards behind the beach there was a parking area, room for a half dozen cars and a public restroom, all squashed between bramble hedges that gave the neighboring beachfront houses some privacy. I walked towards the black sedan, parked with its hood facing the beach access. The rear door was open, and I watched in disbelief as an agent bundled Dykstra into the car, a protective hand on his head. Harbrough was about to climb in on the other side. I rushed forward.

"What the hell is going on? Where are you taking him?"

"Step back." One of the agents came towards me, his hands outstretched as if to push me away. I dodged around him and grabbed the top of the car door, preventing it from closing.

"He's coming in for questioning about a conspiracy to import illegal goods."

"No! That's ridiculous. Look at him: he was nearly killed trying to expose the man who was doing the smuggling. Tanello's the criminal, not him." I locked eyes across the roof of the car with Agent Harbrough. "Tell them!"

Harbrough looked uncomfortable, but, to his credit, he held my gaze.

"I told you, I spent three months infiltrating that organization. We have to get something out of the operation."

"Sarah," Dykstra's voice rose from inside the car. I shrugged off the restraining hand of the nearest agent, and bent down to listen to him.

"Sarah, call Sherat."

"What?" They were pulling me away. In my panic, I could not think who he meant. The car doors slammed shut, and, spitting sand and gravel, the sedan reversed out of the parking spot and sped away, leaving me staring after it.

Chapter 15

The Seagull Motel where the paramedics obligingly dropped me was several blocks back from the shore in a depressing suburb on the south side of Jacksonville. It consisted of an L-shaped arrangement of rooms, built out of concrete blocks painted off-white. At the angle of the L was the office, distinguished by a red neon sign announcing "vacancy" fighting for attention with the now-brilliant morning sunshine. A couple of older American-built cars in the parking lot indicated that at least some rooms were occupied, but there was no other sign of life. The strip malls that stretched out either side of the motel, and the gas station opposite, were equally dead. It was only then, squinting into the painful light, that I remembered that it was Sunday morning, the quietest time of the week.

My escorts led me into the office, and, after issuing me a tube of antiseptic ointment and some large adhesive bandages, handed me over to the manager. She was massive, with a doughy pale complexion, an aqua polyester leisure suit and white nurse's shoes. I launched into my story: I just needed a place to shower and connect with my bank in Atlanta; I had been rescued at sea, and had lost everything: ID, cell phone, clothes, cash. She showed no sign of believing me, much less of sympathy, but seemed accustomed to having waifs and strays dumped on her doorstep. She walked away in the middle of my narrative and returned with two grocery bags full of clothes.

"See if something in here'll fit." Her monotone suggested she had heard it all before. I dreaded what I would find in the bags - her XXL cast-offs and dingy underwear – but I lucked out with an extra small but stretchy black tank top, fashionably threadbare jeans, a grey hoodie and too-large flip-flops. I'd wash out my own underpants, thank you very much. Armed with the clothes and the key to #3, I was suddenly reluctant to leave the manager's drab office for solitude in an equally drab motel room. She might not be my instant best friend, but the plus-sized lady with the neutral affect was infinitely better than what was waiting behind door number three. I was scared that once I was alone I would not be able to keep the demons away. Even teetering on the edge of extreme exhaustion, I wouldn't be able to avoid reliving the entire nightmare, overlain with my piercing new anxiety about Dykstra. I shifted from foot to foot for a moment, looking for an excuse to stay in the office.

"The coffee's free, if you want." The manager gestured at the Mr. Coffee machine, and I wandered over to pour a cup. It was treacle-black and smelt of burnt dust. I knew I would not drink it.

"So, is there a phone in the room?"

"Yes. Local calls are free; long distance billed to the room." She scowled up at me. "No Wi-Fi, and the spa's closed for repairs." It took me a minute to get she was making a joke. I tittered half-heartedly.

"Well, I guess I'll be ….." I opened the door, wincing at the brightness. I looked back, but the manager's head was already bowed down behind the counter, her attention reclaimed by whatever she had been doing before my arrival.

The motel was not my selection. The lone FBI agent remaining in the parking lot after Dykstra was driven away, had warned me self-importantly to keep him apprised of my location. He was evidently not happy at being the one left behind to deal with me, and was reluctant to answer any questions, hiding behind law enforcement jargon vaguely familiar from TV shows. I wasn't sure why they weren't taking me in for questioning too, but after all, it wasn't as if I could skip town without cash, credit card or even shoes.

"Mr. *Deekster* is helping us with our enquiries. He'll be accorded all appropriate rights – for an alien."

It occurred to me then why they had taken him and not me. As a non-citizen, Dykstra's rights (to remain silent, to an attorney, all those familiar benefits secured for us by a small-time Mafia hood named Miranda) might not be guaranteed. It took considerable determination on my part, summoning up as much *hauteur* as possible, given my bedraggled state, to get the agent to even reveal the address of the FBI office to which Dykstra had been taken.   It was in the Federal Building in downtown Jacksonville, sharing space with the federal district court, and a few other federal government agencies.

"He's a journalist, you know. He won't reveal his sources." My parting shot fell flat. The agent was already turning away to talk quietly into his phone.

The room was as I expected: a symphony in beige. I snowshoe-ed over the stained carpet in my too-large flip-flops and hovered a moment before deciding to risk sitting on the bedspread. I slumped there for a few moments, challenging my fuddled brain to tell me what to do next. I had not thought to ask for a no-smoking room, if they even had such a thing, and cigarette odor permeated the furnishings. I got up again to inspect the bathroom: basic but clean, graying towels that smelled of chlorine, and the tiniest complimentary shampoo and soap that I had ever seen. My shoulders sagged for a moment, before I reminded myself how much better this third rate motel room was than the luxury yacht from which I had barely escaped with my life. I shrugged off self-pity and started to formulate a plan of action.

The first priority was a shower, then I needed funds. With money I'd be able to get transportation, clothes, phone, everything I needed to work on getting Dykstra free, and both of us back to Atlanta. I pulled off my salt-stained T-shirt, and peeled down my ruined sweatpants, careful not to scrape my bandaged burns. The meager trickle produced by the shower head meant I was in no danger of dislodging the gauze pads over my wounds. I managed a kind of half-shower, half-sponge bath, and used up the entire shampoo allowance on my hair. Still feeling shaky but much more human, I wound a towel around my waist in a sarong, and put on the tank top. It was tight enough to serve as a substitute bra. I rinsed out my underpants, and left them to dry in a shaft of sunlight.

Getting my bank's 24 hour emergency telephone number out of Information was a labyrinthine effort, but the struggle did not end there.

"For transfers, press or say one; for your balance, press or say two, ... To speak to an operator, press or say nine." But no matter how hard I pressed or how clearly I enunciated "NINE!" the system merely threw me back to the beginning of the litany. I cursed the day I had opted for a local community bank, rather than one of the megalithic giants, although who knew whether their Sunday service was any better? After fifteen wasted minutes, I despaired of Clairmont Federal Bank, and phoned American Express. This sounded more promising. Within only a couple of menu choices, I was reporting my lost or stolen card to a real-live, amazingly friendly and intelligent-sounding woman. If she had been in the room with me, I would have kissed her on both cheeks.

"Would you like that replacement card delivered to you by overnight mail, or will you pick it up at our local American Express office?"

"I'll pick it up. Where's your Jacksonville, Florida, office?"

I wrote down the address, and was mentally high-fiving myself when I caught the tail end of her speech.

"…….when the office opens at ten a.m. tomorrow."

"Tomorrow?" I squeaked. "You mean the office isn't open today?"

"No, it's closed Sundays, but your card will be waiting for you tomorrow, Monday."

A full day and night in this fleapit. Oh, well, it couldn't be helped.

"You'll just have to present a picture ID—"

"But I don't have a picture ID. I lost that as well!" I wailed. Suddenly, my friend and savior turned frosty.

"The card can't be released to you unless you can show a picture ID. Those are the rules."

I hung up, then sat and stared at the phone as I tried to think of another number to call. It was no use; I had stored my address book to my Blackberry, the same Blackberry that was now somewhere on the high seas, tucked into a side pocket of my smart little leather backpack, hanging behind the door of the cabin I had so briefly occupied on board the *Glissando.* Like everyone else in the civilized world, I had come to rely on its storage device, and barely even bothered to memorize my own phone number, let alone those of friends, neighbors or work associates. In any case, who *would* I call to ask for help? My acquaintances all knew me as professional, polished, self-confident and self-reliant. I was reluctant to expose my current predicament to them, and uncertain of what reaction I could expect if I did.

Careless of germs, I fell back onto the bed, ready to give way to depression, when I remembered a number I had used recently enough to have it still traced faintly on my brain. I sat up again and pulled the motel-provided pad and leaky ballpoint towards me. Only the last two digits were uncertain: seven three, or three seven? I wrote it both ways, deciding to try each in turn.

"Gerardo, it's me." Thank God he picked up. "I'm so sorry to call on a Sunday, but," I took a deep breath. "I need your help."

"*No problema*, Sarah. What you need?"

"Do you remember where the spare key to my house is hidden?"

I explained quickly what I needed and where it was: my stash of cash, a credit card I rarely used, my laptop - "*Che*? Oh, *si*, the computer," – my passport and clothes.

"Perhaps Serafina could help? Pick out some clothes for me, I mean? Do you think she would? That would be great. But, Gerardo, there's more. I'm in Jacksonville. It's in Florida. I hate asking you this, but I need you to bring me the stuff here."

There was a pause. I had gone too far. I bit my lip in mortification, waiting for Gerardo to stumble out of the conversation, hiding behind his poor English to save my face.

"Sure, I know Florida; I work citrus there when I come north. I drive your car, yes?"

"Yes! The keys are on the hook in the kitchen, the tank's full. Take I-75 south, then I-16 and—"

"I-95. Yes, I go this way before. Where in Jacksonville?"

I gave him the Seagull Motel's address, and told him to drive safely.

"Thank you so, so much." As I put the phone down, great round tears of gratitude and relief ran down my cheeks. For once, I didn't fight them but gave way to the tide of emotion that swept over me. After a while my sobs subsided. Feeling drained but somehow cleansed, I went into the bathroom to splash cold water on my face and turn, finally, to Dykstra's request that I contact Lelana's father. I puzzled over how to reach him.

Sherat, yesterday at least, was in Atlanta. I knew that Muslim custom demanded prompt burial of the dead. Perhaps he was already on his way back to the Middle East, having held his daughter's funeral in Atlanta. He could not fly to Jordan direct; he would need to change planes in Paris or London, and those flights did not leave Atlanta until the late afternoon. Or he could fly via Washington or New York. There was one person who might know: Mahmet Barouk, the Jordanian Consul-General.

Exhaustion was closing in on me. I had snatched only moments of sleep in the last twenty-four hours, but I was determined to make this last effort before I crawled between the sheets to sleep away the remaining hours until Gerardo's arrival. I secured the twenty-four-hour number for the Jordanian Embassy in Washington without too much difficulty, but had little hope that I'd get through to Barouk, given the run-around I had been given when I had called during regular business hours. However, the Sherat name seemed to act as an "Open, Sesame!" Within a few minutes, I was transferred to what I guessed from the background noise was Consul Barouk's cell phone.

"Wait a minute. Let me get somewhere quiet." A pause. "That's better. What did you say?"

"Pieter Dykstra asked me to call Mr. Sherat. He needs his help. Can you tell me where to reach him?"

I could hear Barouk mulling it over, but after all it was only a couple of days since he was pleading with me to meet with Lelana's father.

"He's staying at the Ritz-Carlton in Atlanta. He was planning to leave the country this evening, if he can get the authorities to release the body, but I doubt if he's checked out yet."

After thanking Barouk, I disconnected, and made yet another call to Information for the Ritz-Carlton's number. I was familiar with the hotel on Peachtree Street downtown, although I had never stayed there. The public rooms were quietly elegant; the bar was dark and clubby, and the dining room had won awards for its cuisine. As I waited to be connected, I amused myself with the contrast between my drab surroundings and what I imagined

Sherat's suite was like: fresh flowers, Egyptian cotton sheets and towels four times the size and thickness of the one I was wearing.

The accented voice that finally answered was not Sherat's, and it took some insistence on my part to get to speak to him.

"Mr. Sherat, this is Sarah McKinney, Pieter Dykstra's friend. We met yesterday at the airport."

"Yes, I remember. What can I do for you, Miss McKinney?"

"It's Pieter. He's being questioned by the FBI in Jacksonville. He – we were on the trail of Lelana's killers but— well, we had to be rescued, and I think the FBI somehow think he's involved in the smuggling. He wanted me to call you." I finished lamely, realizing how ridiculous it all sounded. Sherat had just lost his daughter, and he probably blamed Dykstra for her death. Why would Dykstra think Sherat would help?

"Where is he being held?"

I gave him the address of the Federal Building in Jacksonville, and he asked me to hold. I heard muttered conversation in Arabic. Then the man who had first picked up the phone spoke.

" Mr. Sherat thanks you for the information. Goodbye."

"But will he help?" I was speaking to dead air. The man who I assumed was the same lackey who accompanied Sherat at the airport, had already hung up. I had done all I could for the time being. I calculated it would take Gerardo at least five hours to reach me. When he arrived, I would check out of the motel and head downtown to the Federal Building to see about getting Dykstra released. With my laptop, I'd have access to the necessary legal resources and connections. My confidence that I would succeed was growing. Now what I needed above all was sleep. I set the clock-radio alarm for one-thirty pm, ratcheted up the window air conditioner to high, and, still wondering whether its deep rumble would keep me awake, fell effortlessly into a deep sleep.

Chapter 16

*She was floating just under the surface of the water, flesh deathly
white except for blue-ish eyelids and lips. Long hair streamed and
eddied around her head, washing over the face and upper torso
like a veil. I leant down to grasp the body but all I came away with
was handfuls of lustrous black hair. I shook it off in disgust; the
hair felt slimey and alive, like so many skinny snakes in my hands.
Behind me, someone was laughing, a tinny, mechanical laugh. I
reached into the water again, but this time I leant over too far. I
was falling forward, and as I did so, I recognized it was Lelana
lying there like Ophelia in the Burne-Jones painting, swaying
gently in the water. Still I kept falling, and still the laughter kept
sounding above and behind me, rapid bursts of jarring sound ...*

.... that resolved into the alarm buzzer on the clock-radio.
I lay there for a moment before locating the "off" switch,
deliberately slowing my breathing, and staring around the motel
room as I shook off the nightmare, reassembled my present reality,
and organized the next steps in my mind. Gerardo would arrive
soon, with money, my car, my laptop and, I hoped, some decent
clothes.

I dragged myself out of the bed and into the bathroom. I
located my now-dry underpants and pulled on the charity bag jeans
and hoodie. I splashed cold water on my face, then drained two

155

plastic cupfuls of tap water, wincing at the chlorine flavor. I finger-combed my hair into some semblance of style. The noisy AC unit had done its work and the room was cool, bordering on icy. I took a deep breath and emerged into the blinding light and blessed warmth of a fall Florida afternoon.

I needed food. I had no alternative but to throw myself on the mercy of the manager again.

"My friend is on his way to pick me up with cash to pay for the room and everything, but I wondered, while I'm waiting, if you could loan me ten dollars to get something to eat. I haven't eaten since yesterday, and I'm starving ...." I lost steam in face of her implacable expression. I had seen store window mannequins with more mobile features than hers. I sensed that more pleading would be counterproductive, so I waited.

She shuffled to the back of the office and returned with a coupon.

"This'll get you breakfast at Denny's. It's a block up. You'll be able to see your friend arrive from there." The way she said "friend" suggested disbelief, but I wasn't going to protest.

"Thanks. I really appreciate it."

I was on my way out the door when she called me back.

"Here. Give this for a tip. Those girls work hard." She held out a dollar bill. There was a heart buried somewhere under those massive breasts. I smiled and thanked her again.

The coupon entitled me to breakfast "any time": two eggs, hash brown potatoes or grits, and two strips of bacon or a sausage pattie. I opted for over easy, hash browns and bacon, along with wheat toast. I devoured the lot, plus three cups of coffee only marginally better than the stuff back at the motel. I couldn't remember any meal tasting quite so good, and was sorry I didn't have more than a dollar to give the cheerful black teenager who served me.

I sauntered back to the motel, and arrived in the forecourt in time to see my dark blue Honda pull up to the office.

"Gerardo!" He turned and waited by the driver's door while I hurried over to him. There was an awkward pause. Everything in me wanted to hug him hard, but I knew this would only embarrass him, so I contented myself by beaming my brightest smile and repeating my thanks and appreciation.

"I don't know what I would have done without you. You've saved my life!"

He shrugged and looked at his feet, eager to change the subject.

"I use forty bucks to buy gas. Here is two hundred ten." He pulled the tightly rolled bills out of his pocket and gave them to me. "Serafina help me with clothes, and other things." He gestured into the car.

"Hey, you must have driven straight through. Go get something to eat. I can recommend the Denny's up the street. I'll go change and settle up here, then come and find you, OK?" I tried to hand him back a twenty, but he jammed his hands in his pockets and shook his head.

"I'm OK. I stay here with the car."

There was no point arguing. I grabbed the duffel bag out of the back seat, and headed over to Number Three. As I opened the door, I glanced back. Gerardo was lounged against the car, his face tipped up to the sun. I gulped back a surge of emotion. How did I deserve a friend like him?

***

Although it was Sunday, the security checkpoint in the lobby of the Federal Building was manned and active. I relinquished my computer bag to the maw of the x-ray machine, then proceeded without problems through the metal detector. This time, I had had no difficulty in persuading Gerardo to wait in a nearby coffee shop while I attempted to spring Dykstra. Asking him to accompany me to the FBI's offices would be like inviting Daniel to revisit the lion's den.

"FBI's on the third floor, right?" I asked as I reclaimed my bag.

The security guard nodded without comment, and went back to his paperback. So much for the War on Terror and Orange Alert: all you needed to get in here was a confident attitude and the right clothes. I mentally called down yet more blessings on Serafina, who had gone about her task of packing my emergency wardrobe with a style and intelligence that made me think there was a fashion career waiting for her somewhere. Amongst other outfits in the duffel bag, I found my favorite "law suit": charcoal grey, narrowly tailored, and the perfect pair of classic black pumps with just enough of a platform to make my five foot three look imposing. She even had the foresight to throw some make-up essentials into a zip-lock baggie, along with a tub of hair glop that magically turned my air-dried frizz into sleek and shiny. I was not sure what reception I was going to get from law enforcement, but at least I felt dressed for the occasion.

What I was not prepared for was the empty silence of the third floor. The double glass doors facing me announced in black lettering, "Federal Bureau of Investigation - Jacksonville Division." There appeared to be no one in the lobby behind them. I pushed at the doors, half-expecting them to be locked, but they yielded and I walked forward into a bland reception area. There was a brown tweed-covered sofa to the left, fronted by a coffee table. A line of curvy plastic chairs were to the right, under an attractively framed mirror. Straight ahead was a desk with a phone on it, obviously where a receptionist sat during business hours. But at three p.m. on a Sunday afternoon, there was no one, and no sound from any offices beyond. A photo of Special Agent in Charge Nestor Salazar was mounted on the wall behind the desk; I did not recognize this handsome man with a blindingly white smile as participating in the glum group that had met us at dawn on the beach.

I scanned the surface of the desk to see if there were instructions for out-of-hours visitors, but there was nothing. I picked up the telephone handset and heard a dial tone, but not knowing what extension to dial, I replaced it. A door, equipped with a key pad that persuaded me it would not open without the appropriate code, presumably led into other working areas. I felt silly knocking on it, but could think of nothing else to do. My knock made a muffled thud on the solid steel door. I imagined it was inches thick. In any event, no one came.

Confused about what to do next, I wandered over to the mirror, and examined my make-up, running a wetted finger over my brows, pulling at wisps of my errant bangs. I froze in mid-primp, with the sudden realization that this was probably a two-way mirror. Was that a sound? I leapt back as if burned, then trying to repair my dignity, I sauntered over to the couch, sat down and picked up a section of Friday's Wall Street Journal which was strewn across it. I looked at the headlines without taking anything in.

I was just deciding to descend again to the lobby, and have the security guards down there call up to announce me, when the door to the interior opened, and a woman in khakis and pale blue shirt entered.

"Can I help you?"

"I'm here to see – I mean, my name is Sarah McKinney; I'm an attorney. I represent Pieter Dykstra. He was brought here this morning, and—"

"Yes, of course. Follow me." She smiled warmly, as she led the way through the door into a corridor lined with glass-fronted offices. "I hear y'all had a miserable night of it. How're you doing now?"

I was confused by her friendliness. I had dressed for battle, and prepared myself as well as possible by mentally reviewing my second year law school Criminal Procedure class. I was pretty confident that they couldn't hold Dykstra without charging him, but I had never practiced criminal law. Although I was relieved not to have to cite authority for my presence here, I still suspected a trick.

We passed a row of offices, all empty, and came to another key-pad protected door. The agent tapped in a code, passed through, and then opened a door to the right. I was momentarily blinded by the sun streaming through the floor-to-ceiling window, then I saw Dykstra seated at a table to the left. I stood silently, taking him in, as the agent retreated gracefully, closing the door behind her.

He had dark purple-red circles round his eyes, highlighted by white butterfly band-aids on his eyebrows. That, and the still-swollen mouth, gave him the appearance of a circus clown. His grin was lopsided but still managed to flip something over inside me.

"Are you OK?"

"Sarah! I'm so glad to see you!"

We spoke over each other, then, laughing in relief, stumbled into each other's arms.

"How have they treated you? Are they charging you with anything? Have you had anything to eat? Did you get a chance to rest?—"

"Sarah, Sarah, it's alright. I'm fine. Yes, they questioned me pretty hard to start, then they got the report from the Coast Guard, and, I guess, Harbrough's debrief."

I stood back to scan him head-to-toe. Although his face was a mess, it was washed clean. They had substituted a black T-shirt with "FBI" emblazoned in white, for the bloodied and torn shirt he had been wearing when I last saw him.

"Tell me everything, from the moment you left the beach."

He explained that, although initially they seemed to suspect him of being part of Tanello's organization, or at least complicit in the diamond smuggling, they had done an about-face mid-morning. As Harbrough had anticipated, the Coast Guard party that boarded the *Glissando* had found no illegal activity. Marco's body had disappeared, and there was no obvious sign of violence. Tanello had done a good job of seeming surprised that his crew had abandoned ship while he was sleeping, and was apparently grateful for the Coast Guard's intervention. Had it not been for Arun and Paul emerging bleary-eyed on deck, Tanello probably would not have mentioned that Dykstra and I were also missing, but the young Arabs were persistent in their questions, and Tanello reluctantly agreed to a more thorough search of the vessel.

Although the crew quarters had been cleared out, mine and Dykstra's belongings were still in our cabins. This left Tanello struggling to come up with a better explanation than that we might have decided to leave with the crew. Even Ingrid was woken up and interrogated, but whether her memory of the night's activity had been obliterated by drugs, or she was too scared of Tanello to speak up, she remained silent. A detachment from the Coast Guard vessel was left on board to navigate the *Glissando* back to Hilton Head for further investigation. However, it looked unlikely that Tanello would be held accountable for anything.

"Do you think Lelana's father used some influence on your behalf? I spoke to him, but he didn't promise to intervene. In fact, he really didn't say anything much."

Dykstra shrugged.

"I doubt his contacts could do anything with the FBI, at least not this quickly. My point in asking you to call him was to let him know about Tanello. He'll work out that Tanello is the

American end of the smuggling chain, and that Tanello is responsible for Lelana's death. Then perhaps he'll be motivated to use his influence back in the Middle East to expose the criminal connections used in hiding assets." He frowned, lost in his own thoughts for a moment, then changed the subject. "So, can we go now?" Dykstra was amazingly chipper, considering what he had been through. He mentioned that he'd eaten a sandwich and then grabbed a couple of hours' sleep before my arrival.

"Yes!" I opened the door to find the female FBI agent a couple of feet away, leaning against the wall examining her fingernails. She bounced upright.

"OK. Ready to go?" Her smile reached up to crinkle the corners of her eyes. I thought her super-friendly attitude signaled "don't sue me for a civil rights violation," but I let it pass. "I'll just need an address where y'all can be reached, just in case we need anything else."

Dykstra looked at me questioningly.

"He'll be staying with me," I said firmly. "We're leaving for Atlanta immediately." I gave her my address, email and phone number, ignoring her single raised eyebrow suggesting that this was a more intimate attorney-client relationship than was normal.

We found Gerardo in a mostly deserted Starbucks down the street from the Federal Building. After introductions were made, I slid into the booth opposite the two men. As I looked from one to the other, a warm feeling I identified as contentment swept over me, and I couldn't resist the corners of my mouth lifting in a grin. Here were the two men in my life, about the same age, but so different in other ways. In spite of his battered face and ridiculous FBI T-shirt, Dykstra still looked like a sophisticated European. The hands gave him away: smooth and well-groomed, surprisingly delicate for a big man. And of course the fact that he had opted for an espresso: I knew Europeans never drank milky coffee after noon. Gerardo's hands, in contrast, were those of a working man, with calluses and scars, stubby fingers wrapped around the paper cup of drip coffee.

I felt so lucky to have them both in my life. I almost burst out laughing. Here you are, Sarah McKinney: independent, determinedly single and professionally neutral, handing your heart over to a rootless foreign journalist, and your trust to an undocumented alien.

Dykstra caught my eye and smiled back. "What is so funny?"

I shook my head. "It's nothing. Just glad it's all over, I guess."

He looked at me unblinkingly then, holding my gaze as the smile drained from my face like water from the tub.

"What is it, Pieter?"

"I'm afraid that it's not over. Tanello could come after us. He may be convinced I don't have the diamonds, but .... we know too much."

"Surely he'll lay low; he must realize the FBI's on his trail."

"Maybe . . . I just don't know if we're safe."

Gerardo had been looking idly out of the window. At the word "safe," his head snapped around, and he looked hard at Dykstra.

"Sarah is not safe?"

Much as I appreciated his concern for me, I didn't want Gerardo engaging in some *machismo* competition with Dykstra on who could better protect me.

"It's OK, Gerardo. The Coast Guard has him right now, and the FBI is tracking him. Let's just go home." The warm feeling of connection I had experienced a moment before had been replaced by a sick cramping in my stomach. All I wanted now was to be back in my own little house, doors locked, familiar things around me. The tiredness that purpose – getting Dykstra out of the FBI's grasp - had kept at bay was drowning me again.

"Let's go home," I repeated.

.

Chapter 17

After the inevitable perfunctory squabble about who was the least exhausted and therefore should drive, I overruled the guys' objections and eased carefully into the driver's seat. After all, it was *my* car. I found a position where, with pelvis tilted, I could minimize the pressure on my gauze-padded burns. Dykstra painfully folded his large frame to crawl past the front seat into the back, then Gerardo hunched into the passenger seat.

It was just after five o'clock, but, being Sunday, the traffic was light. I headed cautiously out of downtown Jacksonville, and onto the interstate. We didn't speak. Soon, over the engine noise, I could hear soft snoring coming from the back seat. Gerardo remained awake, scowling at the cars and trucks ahead of us. I assumed his silence and his dour expression meant he was suspicious of Dykstra, the man who had taken me from his protection and exposed me to harm.

The sun was low in the sky to our left. Within an hour it would be dark, with the sudden transition from day to night that characterized Florida's southern latitude. The refrigerated trucks lumbered northwards on I-95 with their freight of salad stuffs, strawberries, and all the other out-of-season crops northerners craved through the cold months. Most of the car traffic was coming the other way. The headlights of snowbirds from Montreal and Philadelphia, heading south for the winter, swept rhythmically across the windshield. We crossed the state line into Georgia, and rolled on towards the interchange with I-16 west of Savannah.

Somewhere near Brunswick, Gerardo also nodded off, and I was alone with my thoughts. Over the last couple of weeks, a tornado had picked me up, and sent me spinning out of control into a different life than the well-ordered, carefully-constructed existence I had enjoyed for several years. I was Dorothy in The Wizard of Oz, following the yellow brick road to God knows where. That was one way of looking at it. Another was that I was subconsciously looking to shake things up, that I had willingly stepped into the unknown to escape the predictability that I had embraced in contrast to my chaotic childhood. Maybe not so subconsciously. After all, I had made choices almost from the first. Perhaps I could not have avoided the bullet that grazed my arm in the hotel, but I could have declined Dykstra's invitation to meet, not accepted the gift of the sphinx, not called him when the sphinx was stolen. Above all, I could have followed my usual cautious approach to men, and not given in to the powerful attraction I felt for Dykstra.

So, what happens now? What do I *make* happen? The old Sarah, the one in tight control of her life, would take Dykstra to bed, then, in the morning, tell him firmly goodbye. I could then immerse myself in work, resume a healthy exercise routine, and start down the list of home and garden improvement ideas I had drawn up. I suspected Gerardo would approve of that.

Or I could make a grab for love, no matter how physically or emotionally dangerous that might be. I was forty years old. If I left it much longer, the shell around my heart would require a sledge hammer to crack. I might never get the chance to share my life with someone, if I sent Dykstra away.

We were on the interminable stretch of I-16 between Savannah and Macon; exits were few and far between. I needed to pee, and besides, chasing the circle of thoughts around my brain was tiring me out. I reached over to gently shake Gerardo's arm.

"I'm going to take the next exit and fill up. Could you take over the driving?"

"*Si,*" Gerardo blinked hard to clear his eyes of sleep. "Is two miles," indicating the roadside sign.

Dykstra woke when we pulled into the pumps. We all visited the restrooms, restocked on water and candy, and rearranged ourselves in the car. I took the backseat this time, and was soon in the restless doze that is all that I can achieve in a moving car, at least one as cramped as the backseat of a two-door Honda Accord. I dropped off for a few minutes, random dream images strobed by highway lights playing on my eyelids, only to jerk awake, drool leaking from my mouth and a crick in my neck. At some point, I was aware of low voices speaking Spanish. Naturally, Dykstra spoke Spanish too. I smiled to myself, wondering what the men in my life were saying to each other. Probably talking soccer, I concluded, then drifted off again.

***

We parked in the street to allow Gerardo to reverse his truck out of my driveway where he'd left it that morning. It was late. The neighborhood was silent, streetlights gleaming off the wet pavement. I shivered as I got out of the car to walk Gerardo over to his truck. I would need to turn on the furnace as soon as I got in the house. That delightful respite between air-conditioning and heating systems was definitely over.

"Tell Serafina thanks too, Gerardo. I'm going to send you a check tomorrow, first thing." I had already asked him to bill me for his time and Serafina's, in an attempt to put their extraordinary generosity on a business footing that might restore the easy-going, hands-off relationship we had always enjoyed. He just shrugged and continued his minute inspection of a ding in the truck's passenger door. He seemed suddenly reluctant to leave. I waited, nervous that he was going to say something critical of Dykstra, and reprove me for getting involved with such a man. I was already getting up a head of steam – none of your business, your rescue doesn't give you a right to interfere in my private life – when he finally spoke.

"That guy . . . ." with a nod of the head indicating the front door where Dykstra had disappeared. "Pieter . . . ." Here it comes, I thought. "He OK guy. I think he . . . . "He was searching for the right English word, still avoiding my eye and obsessively rubbing his thumb over the nicked paint on the truck door. "I think he want you happy. "

I was waiting for the 'but'. Gerardo finally faced me squarely, and grinned his rare snaggle-toothed smile. There was a hint of wickedness in it. "You gotta be happy, Sarah. Is more important than . . ." He gestured vaguely at the house and the well-kept street. "Go, be happy."

With a wave that was almost a benediction, he opened the door and swung up into the driver's seat. Before I could formulate any reply, he had fired up the engine and was backing down the driveway, exhaust belching smoke. The genteel silence of a suburban Sunday night was split by the raucous rumble and clang of Gerardo's ancient, hard-used truck, as he accelerated away down the street.

What had Gerardo and Dykstra talked about as the miles rolled out behind us, and I dozed in the back seat? What had changed Gerardo's doubts about Dykstra into admiration and support? I shook my head in wonderment. Men! It was a club with a secret handshake we women could never learn. But I inwardly hugged myself with pleasure. I didn't like to admit it, but Gerardo's approval meant an awful lot to me. I nearly skipped up the front path, a smile on my face, my tiredness abated for the moment.

Dykstra had taken the few minutes while Gerardo and I had been talking outside to turn on a couple of table lamps and assemble a tray with glasses and a bottle of my "house" red wine. He was placing the tray on the low table in front of the sofa when I entered.

"Is this OK?" He indicated the wine.

"Lovely. Let me turn the heating on." I headed for the short hallway outside my bedroom where the thermostat was located. I was still wearing my business suit and heels. From long habit, I kicked off my shoes and started unbuttoning my jacket as I went. Dykstra caught up with me as I was peering at the heating controls in the near darkness of the hallway. He slid his arms around me from behind and peeled off my jacket. I was wearing only a bra underneath. I turned towards him. His eyes held a question that I answered with my lips, brushing his mouth gently, teasingly, until we reached for each other more urgently.

He gripped my upper arm, and I lurched back instinctively. "Ow!"

"I'm so sorry! Let me see." He led me back into the light of the living room, and examined the gauze pad, about four inches square, that was taped over the bullet scar and its circle of burns.

"What's this? I thought the bullet wound had healed." His mouth turned grim. "Tell me what he did to you."

I told him as briefly and unemotionally as I could how Tanello had used a lighted cigarette to try and get me to tell him what I did not know: where the diamonds were. I had no wish to dwell on it, but I knew he would not let me shrug it off with an "I'm fine."

He held my eyes for a long moment. I was amazed to see the glint of tears. Then he sighed and looked away, still holding my hand.

"Sarah, I am so, so sorry. I didn't even ask you before, just thinking of myself and the damn story. It's my fault. So stupid, so selfish! I should not have involved you—"

"Hey, wait a minute. You didn't drag me into it by my hair." I smiled at him, speaking gently to try to regain the intimacy we had shared a minute earlier. "I wanted to be with you. I *want* to be with you …"

He looked back at me then, his face still serious. He reached a finger to my jawline and slowly traced it down to the point of my chin, up to my lips, my eyebrows. His touch was as soft as a butterfly. It was as if he was learning my face. Then he leant in and kissed my throat, again with tenderness, an unspoken request for forgiveness.

"It's cold in here. Come to bed," I whispered.

We made love gently, taking care to avoid each other's hurt places. For a first time, it felt strange. There was none of the hunger and urgency, even violence, with which I had plunged into other sexual affairs. I felt sure that Dykstra and I would find that physical passion in time, but for now, this was enough, more than enough. Like coming home, a feeling of safety, of being cherished. A feeling that was at once familiar and totally new to me. I wanted to hold on to it, to ride it slowly into sleep, but just as I was conscious of the thought, and of Dykstra's rhythmic breathing against my hair, I felt a hard little nut of self-consciousness keeping me awake.

It was always this way with me. It was as if my body produced antibodies that fought the post-coital endorphins gently meandering through my bloodstream. But it wasn't my body resisting; it was my mind: the voice that told me I could not be loved, did not deserve love, could not trust love. The damage had been done so long ago and far away that I no longer had a particular memory of it. Scar tissue had covered it over, just like in time the bullet's track and the cigarette burns would be obscured and fade into the surrounding flesh. But always, deep under the surface, the wound persists. I've read the books, gone to therapy, done the work, followed all the prescriptions for recovery, but in my heart, or gut, or some other dark corner of selfdom that reason does not penetrate, the damage remains. Even in a moment of what should be unadulterated contentment, there is something, just out of sight, just a shadow. A child's fist clenched around a stone. The color and shape of the stone is lost, but the pain of its point against the palm of my hand comes back to remind me.

I moved slightly towards the edge of the bed so that Dykstra's sleep would not be disturbed by my sobs.

Chapter 18

When I finally fell asleep, I slept hard. I was unaware of Dykstra leaving the bed, and woke past nine o'clock to the smell of coffee brewing and the murmur of NPR from the kitchen. I couldn't understand how I had slept through my default seven a.m. alarm, until I checked and found that some thoughtful soul had disabled it. I stretched under the sheet, sounding out my body for pain. Surprisingly, there was only an itchy tightness on my buttocks and upper arm, and at my wrists where the ligatures had cut into my skin. The wounds were healing.

I wondered cynically what "morning after" personality Dykstra might assume when I ventured out for the coffee. Would he strut and preen like a rooster, urging compliments on his sexual performance, pouting if I didn't tell him the earth moved? I'd met *that* fellow before. Or worse, the commitment-phobe who can't meet your eye, and mumbles something about an early meeting as he heads out the door. Deciding to postpone the inevitable let-down, I crept into the bathroom for a shower.

When I emerged, decidedly unglamorous in a toweling robe, wet hair combed straight back, I nearly ran into him. He was carrying a loaded tray.

"Good morning. I was planning breakfast in bed, but if you'd rather eat out here …?"

The grin, even with bruises along his jaw and butterfly bandages holding his eyebrows together, had its now-familiar effect on me. So much for self-protective cynicism. When my insides resumed their customary position, they signaled hunger.

"Mmm, scrambled eggs. Lovely! Well, since you've gone

172

to the trouble of fixing a tray ..." I followed him back into the bedroom.

Later, as I was stuffing sheets into the washer, the doorbell rang. Dykstra was in the shower now, belting out the Toreador chorus from Carmen – so he was a bit of a rooster, after all – and I was not about to open the door without knowing who was on the other side. A scant week ago, Lelana had stood on my porch, her finger on the doorbell. Now she was dead, as was the thug who had accompanied her. I had been kidnapped and tortured, and I suspected I wasn't out of the woods yet.

I hurried into the front bedroom that served as my office. The window offered a clear view of the street. A black limousine blocked my driveway as well as my neighbor's. Tinted glass prevented me from seeing if anyone was inside. I craned sideways to see who was at the front door. On the porch stood a dark-haired man in a business suit. He was turned away from me and I did not recognize him at first. But I did recognize the roll-on case and duffle bag at his feet. I must have let out a whoop, because the man turned my way. It was Paul, the shorter and plumper of the two Middle-Eastern playboys who Tanello had used to lure Dykstra, with me in tow, onto the yacht. He looked awkward in a suit, even though it was well-cut. Like a schoolboy dressed up for a wedding. Somehow, he seemed to have found time for a haircut in the thirty-six hours since I had last seen him on the *Glissando*.

I thumped on the bathroom door.

"Paul's here and he's brought our luggage."

"Is he alone?"

"I don't know."

"Wait for me." A couple of seconds later, Dykstra came out of the bathroom, dripping, with a towel wrapped around his waist. "OK, let's see what he has to say."

I opened the door. "Hello, Paul."

"Hi, Sarah, I've –" He caught sight of Dykstra's torso, purple fading to brown in stripes across his ribcage. "Oh, my God, what happened?"

I lost it. "What do you *think* happened, Paul? Tanello's sidekick Marco worked him over, nearly killed him. You and Arun were the ones that got us on that boat in the first place. Don't tell me you thought Tanello wanted us there to make up a foursome for bridge!"

Paul stood there looking stupid with eyes wide and mouth gaping while I fumed, hands on hips. Dykstra just looked amused.

"Great! You've brought our bags," he said smoothly, attempting to diffuse the tension. "I needed a change of clothes." He bent over the duffel bag, continuing in the same light tone, "Who's in the car, Paul? How did you get Sarah's address?"

"It's my uncle's limo. He sent me with the bags. There's just the driver with me, I don't know his name. The driver's name, not my uncle's." He laughed nervously and prattled on. "He's not really my uncle, though. I just have always called him that since I was a child: Uncle Bashir." He looked from me to Dykstra, as if for approval. "Bashir Sherat? You know, Lelana's father? I told you, Lelana and I grew up together. Boy, was I glad to see him when we got back to Hilton Head!"

"OK, Paul. You'd better sit down and fill us in. I'm just going to put some clothes on. I'll be right back."

Dykstra grabbed his duffel and disappeared into the bedroom. I gestured for Paul to take a seat. I was still seething at the little pipsqueak, but also intrigued. So my call to Mr. Sherat from Jacksonville had produced some results, if only to reunite us with our luggage. I excused myself to put another pot of coffee on. By the time I came back from the kitchen, Dykstra had emerged, dressed in clean jeans and a sweat-shirt.

Under Dykstra's skillful probing, Paul explained everything that had happened since he regained consciousness with a massive headache on Sunday morning to find the U.S. Coastguard in command of the yacht, and Marco, Dykstra and me strangely missing. Tanello warned him, Arun and Ingrid not to answer any questions, then installed himself in a corner of the saloon with a face like thunder.

"He didn't say a word until we got back to port, except to demand to be allowed to call his lawyer. When we docked – it was about two in the afternoon – there was quite a crowd to greet us: a bunch of FBI types with a search warrant, Lou's lawyer, Uncle Bashir – thank goodness - and a guy from the Jordanian Embassy. They made us stay on deck while they searched the whole boat. Ingrid just fell apart. You know, between ourselves, I think that girl has a drug problem. Arun wasn't much better, but the embassy guy got onto the State Department or something, because after a while a car came and took Arun and me, and Uncle and the embassy guy to the Savannah airport. Then Arun and I had to sit in this room with an FBI agent while Uncle worked out a deal."

He paused to sip his coffee. He seemed to be quite enjoying telling his tale, the center of attention, oblivious to my strained expression as I tried to reconcile his naiveté with the near-death experience we had suffered.

"So, what was the deal?" Dykstra prompted.

"Arun was deported – just like that. He flew out last night. Can never come back to the States, which is a bummer. But I got immunity, if I testify in front of this grand jury thing tomorrow. I have to tell them everything I know about Tanello, Marco, well, everything. After that, I'm free to leave. I'm going back with Uncle Bashir to Amman. He wants me to stay with him for a while. I guess I'm like a son to him …" He smirked.

"And what *do* you know?" The casual way Dykstra posed the question did not fool me. He was honing his story, joining the dots, closing the loops. He reminded me of a cat watching a bird, sitting back on my sofa, loose-muscled and still, but with unblinking eyes fixed on his target.

"Well, I don't know if I'm supposed to talk about it. Isn't the grand jury supposed to be secret?"

Dykstra didn't answer the question. Instead he sighed.

"You know, even with your testimony, they may not be able to indict Tanello. There are so many legal loopholes he could squirm through. But if the story gets published, we can put him out of business for sure. Don't we owe that to Lelana?"

I bit my lip to keep from interrupting. Although I thought Paul was a spoilt brat, and blamed him for pulling us into Tanello's orbit, I couldn't help an urge to protect him from Dykstra's blatant manipulation.

Dykstra ignored my doubtful expression. "Let's start with how Tanello knew I'd given the sphinx to Sarah."

"Ah, well, we told him that."

"When was that?"

"It was about a couple of weeks ago, around the end of September. Arun and I were in Paris. His sister's at the Sorbonne. She has a really neat pad on the rue du Bac, but classes hadn't started back up, she was still in Cairo, so we were crashing there. We'd been out clubbing, it was late, and Lelana called in a panic."

Dykstra turned to me. "That must have been the night you came to the apartment in London. She must have waited until I was asleep." He turned back to Paul. "And then you called Tanello?"

"Yeah, right. Well, Arun called, but I heard it all. He passed on Sarah's name and description and that she was flying back to Atlanta the next day. It was Arun's idea to hide the diamonds in the sphinx. He'd used that trick himself before , but he was scared to do it again. That's why he got me to involve Lelana. I didn't want to, but he said it would be fine. She was with you and journalists fly all the time, and they're never searched …."

Paul's voice was rising in his effort at self-justification. Dykstra steered him skillfully back on track.

"So Arun told Tanello how the diamonds were hidden in the sphinx and that Sarah was taking it to Atlanta. Did he – or you – tell anyone else?"

"No! Arun's dad said – I mean, the people who wanted to get the diamonds to Tanello didn't want to know *how* it was done. That was all left to us, and we knew better than to tell anyone else."

"What about Lelana? Did she tell anyone?"

"Who would she tell? No, she was shit-scared, man. It was her first run and it was all screwed up. Tanello told us to tell her to sit tight until he worked something out, then she was to get on a plane to Atlanta and get the diamonds back from you. That's it. Next thing, Lelana's dead."

Dykstra sighed. "But if Tanello didn't recover the diamonds, who did? You're sure no one else knew Sarah had taken the sphinx to Atlanta?"

"Yeah, I'm sure. There was that girl but she didn't speak English –"

"What girl?" Dykstra sat upright on the sofa, his voice sharp.

Paul frowned with the effort of remembering. "Arun picked up a chick that night and brought her back to the apartment." He ducked his head, embarrassed. "She was in Arun's bed when Lelana called. She was Italian or Greek, I think. Anyway, she spoke French, not English. Arun and I spoke in English or Arabic. Lelana too."

"But she heard Arun talking to Lelana. And to Tanello?"

"I don't know, I think she left before we called Tanello. But she was just some random girl. I don't even remember her name. I doubt if Arun does either. Oh, I nearly forgot, Uncle wants you both to come to dinner tonight at the hotel. We can send the limo."

"Hmm?" Dykstra was still working out story angles, so I stepped into the conversation.

"Did he say why he wants to meet us?"

"I think he wants to talk about Lelana. I think he feels guilty about trying to marry her off to that old guy. They're finally going to release the body tomorrow."

The three of us sat quietly for a moment, each holding in our minds the image of the beautiful young woman, and the thought of her violent death.

"Yes, let's have dinner with him, Pieter. He needs to hear that she had good times, that her last months weren't lived in fear."

He looked at me then, the canny reporter gone, just sadness in his eyes. He did feel something for her then, and I loved him for that.

***

I came to the States at age eighteen to take up a scholarship at Rome College, a small, liberal arts school in North Georgia. Miss Munford had unearthed my paternal great aunt's bequest in the struggle to confirm my US citizenship. Aunt Lucinda had sat on the Board of the College for many years and several of the buildings on campus bore her name. Although we had never met, she had provided generously in her will for my undergraduate education. Miss M, for her part, had schooled me rigorously for the intellectual challenge.

Over my four years at Rome, I slowly adjusted to America. However, on that August day in 1990 when I first arrived at Atlanta Hartsfield Airport, I was totally unprepared for the culture shock. At my English high school, I had adopted the protective camouflage of a nerd: shy, studious, plain in dress, self-effacing in posture. In the colorful chaos of Baggage Claim, I

178

must have looked like a Dickensian waif, dressed for an English summer in my oversized beige "mac," as I still called it then, lugging an antique leather suitcase (parting gift from Miss M) through the din and confusion to the sliding glass doors. The afternoon heat and humidity hit me like a brick wall. Reeling with jet lag, I searched for a taxi.

Another shock: the language problem. The cab driver looked at me blankly as I repeated over and over the address of Aunt Lucinda's lawyer's office. I was to get final instructions there for my onward journey to North Georgia. It occurred to me that I had happened on the one cabbie in Atlanta who spoke no English. Close to tears, I finally dug out the correspondence I had received from the law firm of Pennywell & King, and showed him the letterhead.

"Oh, Two Fifty Peachtree Street!"

I thought I said that. Never mind, we were off, hurtling from lane to lane on the expressway north to Downtown, me tensely watching the meter as it clicked through the dollars and cents at a frightening rate. I was grateful to be released after about half an hour of this, with enough currency to meet the total, plus what I thought was a princely two dollar tip. Luckily, I could not understand the driver's comment as he handed me my suitcase.

The Ritz-Carlton Hotel is situated adjacent to the tower that housed the lawyer's office, and in my dazed condition I confused the entrances. In the dim coolness of the hotel lobby with its Turkey rugs, antique side tables and tasteful landscape paintings, the tears finally came. They were kind to me there. The concierge showed me the short-cut through to the office building's atrium; the bellboy helped me identify the correct floor, and insisted on carrying my bag right to the elevator bank. They treated me as if I was a respected guest.

That is why, although it is not the largest or the newest, or now even the most luxurious of Atlanta's hotels, I have a fond place in my heart for the Ritz-Carlton, and I was pleased that Lelana's father was staying there.

I dressed for dinner with particular care in deference to the hotel as well as to Mr. Sherat. I chose a midnight blue silk jersey dress that stopped below the knee, demure at the front with long sleeves and a boat neckline that grazed my collarbone, but with a plunging vee at the back. A pair of diamond studs in my ears, and my beloved Jimmy Choos – black, shiny, strappy sandals – completed the ensemble. Dykstra was appropriately awestruck.

"You look …." His mouth hung open.

"Lovely? Magnificent? Beautiful?" I supplied, teasing.

"Better!" His eyes gleamed and, mock-devilish, he started to prowl towards me.

"Oh, darn, the limo's here!" Laughing, I danced out of his grasp to open the front door.

When Dykstra asked for Bashir Sherat at the hotel desk, we were told he was expecting us, and a bellhop was summoned to show us the way. He steered us past the regular elevators to a discreet corridor where a private elevator whisked us up to the penthouse suite. The door slid open to reveal an anteroom flanked with console tables bearing fragrant white flower arrangements. Double doors stood open ahead of us.

"Welcome." With his hand on his heart, Sherat made a bow, then extended his hand to each of us. I remembered that when we had met at the airport only a few days earlier, he had declined to shake my hand, and indeed had avoided even looking at me. His manner to both of us, though far from effusive, had certainly warmed.

"Hi!" Paul bounced out of the sitting room beyond. "Come on in and have a drink!"

I caught a momentary wince that passed across Uncle Bashir's face, as he gestured for us to enter ahead of him. More white flowers, gold velvet drapes, and inviting sofas upholstered in cream damask facing each other across a low marble-topped table. Several large table lamps threw a quiet glow over all this harmonious luxury.

"I thought we would have dinner here rather than in the restaurant. " Sherat indicated a table set with white linens and glistening crystal. I wondered whether his choice had anything to do with the hotel restaurant where I had been shot, implicating his sister and hurtling me into his daughter's life. Probably not, I decided. An elder statesman like him would avoid public places wherever possible by long-formed habit. "May I offer you a glass of champagne before we are served?"

I suppressed the memory of that other bottle of champagne, warming in a bucket of melted ice in the *Glissando*'s saloon, and nodded my assent. Paul jumped up to tussle with foil, wire and cork. I was surprised, and a little amused, to see him pour only two flutes: for Dykstra and me. Sherat evidently abstained from alcohol, and Paul, however reluctantly, was playing by his uncle's rules.

While we waited for dinner to be brought up, Dykstra and Sherat made small talk, if "small" was an appropriate description of the high level to-and-fro between a seasoned investigative reporter and a statesman with forty years of government service. I felt that Paul and I should whip out pencils and take notes. Libya's Ghadaffi was a "buffoon," his top military leaders would defect at the first sign of an organized insurgency. Assad in Syria was "as cruel as his father but lacking his intelligence." Sherat dodged questions about the Arab-Israeli peace process, except to say that "settlements in the West Bank were a serious impediment." They agreed to differ about whether traditional monarchies in Jordan, Saudi Arabia and the Persian Gulf could withstand pressures to democratize, Dykstra opining that the internet generation with its expectations of transparent and immediate communication of ideas could not be denied, while

181

Sherat felt that a combination of broad-based coalitions and petro-dollars would shore up the status quo.

Servers arranged covered platters on the table and quietly withdrew. We sat down to lamb tajine, subtly spiced with cinnamon and mint, couscous with pine nuts and raisins, and a salad of sharp-tasting greens which complemented the other flavors to perfection. Dykstra and I drank a St. Emilion Grand Cru made from grapes harvested in the last century. It probably cost more than the dress I was wearing, and I nearly wept to see the bottle left one third full. Sherat and Paul drank tea.

Once the dishes were discreetly cleared and we were settled again on the sofas, a sense of expectation hummed around our heads. Sherat had invited us for a reason, and it was not to discuss Middle-Eastern politics. However, he would not be hurried. We watched in silence as he carefully prepared more tea and served it to us in thimble-sized porcelain cups. Then he sat back, steepled his hands in front of his chest, and closed his eyes.

"Tomorrow, I will take my daughter's remains back to Amman for burial. Apparently, she was killed as punishment for losing over a million dollars' worth of diamonds, diamonds that she had agreed to smuggle to the United States on behalf of Arun's father or one of his associates, a highly placed government official in Egypt."

"It was Arun's idea to get Lelana involved," Paul interrupted, drawing a withering glance from his uncle before the older man closed his eyes again and resumed.

"What I don't understand is why. Why did she agree to do it? And more: why did she run away from home, from me, from everything familiar and dear to her. Yes, yes, she didn't want to marry the man chosen for her, I know that now, but why didn't she come to me? I would never have forced her against her will!" Sherat leant forward now, his voice sharp, eyes piercing into Dykstra's. "Tell me what she was thinking."

Dykstra took his time assembling his words. I hoped he would be gentle with the older man. For all his superficial stiffness, Mr. Sherat was struggling with intense emotional loss. It would not be helpful to point out at this moment that his own neglect and the delegation of his daughter's welfare to his sister had pushed Lelana away.

"Lelana had a wonderful appetite for life. She told me she felt trapped in Amman. I think she panicked, and then ran away to London. Once there, maybe her pride prevented her from reaching out to you," Dykstra paused, straightening his shoulders. When he spoke again his voice was less tentative.

"What I can tell you is that Lelana was happy in London. *We* were happy. At least, until just before she left. I put her nervousness then down to the shooting when Sarah was injured, but now I see it was because I had unwittingly given the diamonds to Sarah. I honestly don't know why she agreed to smuggle the gems. I've given it a lot of thought. Perhaps because she wanted money of her own, didn't want to rely on me to support her, and felt she couldn't ask you for money. She was ..... very young."

Paul cleared his throat to speak. I dreaded another self-serving finger-pointing at his former friend Arun, but he surprised me.

"Uncle, remember how she always loved adventures? When we went to the caves at Aqaba? I was too scared to go in, but she wasn't – and she was only about seven. And that big stallion, the Arabian? You said we must not ride him, he was too wild. Well, she tried, and he threw her. She never told you, did she?" Paul's face was alight with memories, and I was pleased to see a shadow of a smile on Sherat's lips.

"Her independent spirit, her love of adventure, I will always remember. Perhaps I must accept the loss as Allah's will." His face darkened. "But her killers must be held accountable. That is your job now. You, Paul, tomorrow you must tell the Americans all you know about Arun's father's scheme, the connection with this criminal Tanello, everything! And Mr. Dykstra, you will publish the story in the newspaper, so everyone knows the names of these evil-doers. Will you both promise?"

Paul and Dykstra solemnly assented, and Sherat gave a deep sigh of relief.

I had contributed little to the conversation all evening. After pausing for a moment to let the intensity around the coffee table dissipate. I repeated the question Dykstra had posed that morning to Paul.

"So who stole the sphinx from my house? It wasn't Tanello or his gang, so who?"

Dykstra and Sherat exchanged significant glances. Dykstra spoke first.

"I can think of two possibilities. What is your theory, Mr. Sherat?"

"I assume you mean Al Qaeda or Mossad?" Dykstra nodded, while my jaw dropped. Sherat continued, "I think we can rule out Al Qaeda. They are not organized for this kind of thing. So that leaves Mossad."

"Israeli intelligence? But they're spies, not jewel thieves! Why would they steal diamonds?" My amazement made me stammer.

"Because they *can*," Dykstra responded. "Mossad's aim is to keep Israel's enemies off-balance. And don't be fooled into thinking the Camp David Accords make Egypt any less of an enemy to Israel than other Arab countries. Stealing the diamonds sends a signal to Mubarak and the other Mid-East power brokers that they can be outsmarted, that Israel's one step ahead all the time."

"But how did Mossad know the diamonds were in the sphinx and that I had the sphinx here in Atlanta?" Even as I articulated the question, I realized the answer. "That girl, the

Italian girl Arun picked up in Paris. She heard Lelana's call to Paul and Arun that night after you gave me the sphinx, and then the call Arun made to Tanello."

"But she didn't speak English or Arabic ......" Paul's voice trailed off, as he understood that he had been duped. "So she was a spy. Just wait until I tell Arun he screwed a Mossad agent!"

"You will have no contact whatsoever with that young man, or any of his associates," Sherat's voice was icy. "Is that understood?"

"Yes, Uncle." Paul wilted into the sofa cushions, while Mr. Sherat stood up, indicating that the evening was drawing to a close. "Paul will call down for the driver. Thank you both for spending the evening with me. Please do not hesitate to call on me if you are ever in Amman, or if you ever need my assistance in any way." He bowed, one hand to his heart again, then escorted us through to the elevator. I didn't imagine I would ever see him again, although I suspected that he would prove a useful future contact for Dykstra. We thanked him for dinner, and I added a final expression of sympathy for his daughter, before the elevator door closed on his tautly held figure.

It had rained while we had been cosseted behind the velvet drapes. Streetlights and headlights reflected off the wet road surface. We sat in silence, hands clasped between us on the back seat, but our faces turned to the side windows. I was thinking how Sherat's formality and correctness barely covered the immense pain of his loss, a loss made even more bitter by the knowledge that he had needlessly driven her away from him in the last months of her life. I wondered what role his sister would play in his household now, and whether Paul could in some small way fill the void in his affections left by Lelana.

We were half way home before Dykstra revealed *his* thoughts.

"Do you think she did it for me?"

"What do you mean?"

Dykstra turned towards me. "I wonder if Lelana agreed to smuggle the diamonds to help me nail the story. I was pushing her to get Paul and Arun to invite me on the Caribbean sailing trip. I didn't know about Tanello then, I just wanted to get closer to Paul and Arun, learn more about their involvement. What if she told Arun she'd bring the diamonds into the States when we came to join the yacht. He'd have to include me on the cruise then."

His face looked haggard as shadow and light passed over it. I searched for words to assuage his guilt but came up empty. After a moment, he turned back to the window. I squeezed his hand, trying to communicate a little comfort. After a while he spoke again.

"You see, if I'm implicated – if she did it for my story – I might not be able to publish. It might be seen as a breach of journalistic ethics."

I felt a chill that made me huddle down into my shawl. I didn't withdraw my hand, although I suddenly wanted to. We didn't speak again until the limo arrived back at my house.

It took me a while to reconcile Dykstra's contradictory revelations about his feelings – or lack of them – for Lelana. I hid myself in the bathroom, stretching out the removal of make-up and brushing of teeth until I thought I had come to terms with them. After all, did I really want a man who was deeply in love with one woman, but who could then fall for another within days of her death? I *had* to trust my gut: we connected, sexually, intellectually, and even emotionally. I was as committed to my career as he was to his. Why not just enjoy each other for as long as it lasted? Resolved to stop the second-guessing, I joined Dykstra in bed.

Chapter 19

As agreed the night before, we walked Paul over to the Federal Building for his two o'clock appointment with the federal grand jury. We didn't expect him to emerge until after five. The plan was to meet him for a debriefing before putting him in a cab for the airport. Mr. Sherat was leaving earlier from the hotel with all the luggage in the limo. He would supervise the formalities of getting Lelana's body through customs and onto the plane. The flight to Paris was scheduled to leave at 7.45 pm. The connection to Amman left Charles De Gaulle the next morning.

Dykstra and I whiled away the time at the CNN Center. It was just a couple of blocks from the Federal Building, but I had only suggested it as a joke. I couldn't imagine that a seasoned journalist would want to join the tourists trailing around faked-up TV studios, or peering through glass at "real" newsrooms, but he had jumped at the idea, and it turned out to be surprisingly interesting. I had never done the tour before. It was the sort of thing Atlanta residents only did with out-of-town guests, and as I never had visitors who were not strictly business, I'd never thought of going.

Our guide took us through a brief history of cable news, explaining how the accelerated cycle – news as it actually happens, twenty-four hours a day – made it ever more important for journalists to get it right; there was no margin for error. I glanced at Dykstra from time to time to see if he was getting bored, but he seemed as fascinated as the rest of us, occasionally nodding his agreement at a point the guide was making. I was gaining an insight into his work life, and an increased respect for his dogged pursuit of "the story."

Of course, there was some silly stuff too. You couldn't expect to hold the interest of a diverse crowd of sight-seers for long with a discussion of journalistic ethics. I played along at being a meteorologist in front of a blue screen, while Dykstra projected extreme weather patterns behind me from the control booth. We ended the tour in the atrium as part of the studio audience for the daily taping of some pundit's show to be broadcast that evening. Dykstra was pretty confident that the host's jokey repartee with audience members would be edited out before airtime. Anyway, neither of us contributed. For me the best part of the whole afternoon was just wandering around hand-in-hand with Dykstra, being a normal couple in the crowd.

We eventually emerged, like moles blinking in the late afternoon sunshine, and made our way over to the plaza in front of the Atlanta Federal Building, a twenty-five storey concrete construction built with an eye to functionality rather than architectural style, unless that style was "Communist-era blockhouse." We had plenty of time to admire it, and the view over the wasteland of parking lots and freeway ramps that surrounded it, because Paul did not appear until a quarter to six. The sun sank into clouds and a chilly breeze whipped up the litter around our feet. The rush hour traffic thickened to an impenetrable snarl. Evidently there was Monday night football at the Georgia Dome, just a few blocks to the north. A steady stream of pedestrians clad in the Falcons' red and black was headed that way. I was impatient to say goodbye to Paul, and get Dykstra back to Decatur for a cozy *diner a deux*.

And, if I could get up the nerve, perhaps a discussion about our future – if we had one, and what it might look like. My resolve to just take things as they came was already weakening. Although I kept reminding myself we had only known each other for a couple of weeks, the intensity of that time and everything we had undergone together cemented us together – at least in my mind. But what was in Dykstra's? I didn't think it was just the sex – although the sex was pretty fantastic – but beyond that I was unsure how he regarded the relationship. He had plunged into it so soon after Lelana's disappearance: was he seeking reassurance, comfort, a confidence boost? In other words, a banal rebound affair. I pushed these thoughts aside as Paul approached us.

"So, how did it go?" Dykstra had talked to Paul at length about what information Paul was able to provide the government that would ensure Tanello's indictment. He wanted to make sure that nothing unexpected came up, and glean as much as he could about how the U.S Attorney's office planned to proceed with the case, before Paul made his escape back to the Middle East under a guarantee of immunity.

"OK, I guess. The guy from the Jordanian embassy is still there, working out the details. I said I had a plane to catch." Then, turning to me, "Hey, there was a black dude there asking if I knew you –"

"What?" Paul's American idioms in a Middle-Eastern accent didn't amuse me.

"Yeah, with the local police, not the FBI. I think he's the detective on the murder case – I mean, Lelana's, you know ….."

"Detective Dobey? Yes, I know him. What was he asking you?"

"Like, why did Lelana come to see you, did I know the guy with her, that kind of stuff. I told him everything I knew. I'm pretty sure they've nailed Marco for the killer. You don't have to worry."

"I'm not." I replied icily. I had to keep reminding myself that Paul was very young. Getting involved in an international criminal scheme was an adventure to him, a real-life video game, even if it had resulted in the death of a childhood friend. Perhaps separated from Arun and the other rich young hoodlums he had been running with, and under Sherat's austere tutelage, he might mature someday into a responsible adult.

Paul peered anxiously at his Tag Hauer.

"Where can I catch a cab? The plane leaves in two hours."

"This isn't New York. You can't just hail a passing cab on the street. We could go back to the hotel. There'll be a line of them there, but honestly, your best bet is MARTA. In this traffic it will take a cab an hour to get to the airport. The train does it in twenty minutes, and Five Points Station is much closer than the Ritz-Carlton anyway."

Paul looked a little green at the idea of taking public transit, and I had to bite my lip to suppress a smile.

"Don't worry, we're going to take the train back to my house from Five Points too. I'll show you how it's done. You'll be quite safe."

Dykstra grabbed Paul's arm and steered him across the street before the lights changed. As we threaded our way through the crowds – tired downtown workers making their way home and ebullient football fans coming the other way – he continued questioning Paul closely about the afternoon's session.

"So did they say whether there's enough to indict?"

"I think so. They have another witness from the *Glissando;* they wouldn't say who but I guess it's either Captain Steve or Ingrid."

Frankly, I didn't think either the gorgeously tanned and toned Steve, or the anorexic addict Ingrid would make stellar witnesses for the prosecution, but maybe cumulatively with Paul's contribution, a case could be made. I was glad I was no longer a member of the cast.

Once we entered Five Points Station, the crowds and the noise increased exponentially, a perfect storm of rush-hour mayhem. Clearly, many of the sports enthusiasts coming up from the trains had started celebrating prematurely. Amongst the red and black regalia of Falcons fans could be seen the green and gold of the visiting team's supporters. Transit police were much in evidence, content for now to just encourage the rival fans to move along out of the station, but keeping an eye open for verbal taunts to escalate into a brawl. Meanwhile the downtown workers, dragging home exhausted after a long day, were losing patience, elbowing any exuberant dawdlers out of the way with unnecessary vehemence.

We fought our way over to the ticket machines, where I purchased three tickets, Paul, predictably, having nothing smaller than a one hundred dollar bill. We edged our way through the turnstiles, and then Dykstra and I prepared to part ways with Paul.

"Look, the escalator to the North-South Line is over there. Just go down and look for the Southbound platform. Make sure the train is going all the way to the airport – that's the end of the line." I took a little pity on him. "It won't be so crowded after the first few stops. You'll be there in plenty of time to catch the plane."

Suddenly, he surprised us by seizing our free hands. As I was already hand-in-hand with Dykstra, the three of us were standing there, buffeted by the passing crowds, like kids in the playground about to play ring-a-ring-a-rosy.

"Sarah! Pieter! I'm so sorry about everything! About Lelana, and the *Glissando* and everything." He seemed genuinely downcast, and I was on the point of saying something blandly comforting when his face brightened. "I know, why don't you both come to Gstadt with me for New Year's? My father has a chalet there, and I'm going to have a big party. It'll be a blast!"

Dykstra laughed. "Maybe. You have a safe flight, and keep in touch, OK?"

With a wave, Paul hurried off towards the North-South line, while we turned to battle our way over to the access for the Eastbound line. I was suddenly light-hearted. With Paul's departure a door swung shut on a dark room where bad things had happened. Now I was starting fresh, and on my own turf. The lurking fear of loss of control, the echo of all my childhood nightmares, had blown away like fog.

I enjoyed this sensation of release for only a few moments. Dykstra's hand slipped out of mine, and when I turned, he was standing stock-still, with his mouth open.

"I just saw him – Tanello! He's … he's going after Paul!" With that, he turned and was swallowed by the crowd. I took a second to absorb what he had said, then fearfully scanned the people around me. But whatever Dykstra had seen from his height of six-foot-something was invisible to me at five-foot- three. All I could see were a mass of jackets, front or back, forming a surrounding hedge. I could only dive between them back the way we had come towards the escalator down which Paul had disappeared.

I was cursing out loud but no one could hear over the din. I cursed Tanello, who I had thought we were done with. And Paul, the bait that had evidently lured Tanello into our ambit again. And, most of all, Dykstra and his never-ending lust for "the story," with no thought for his own safety and that of the people around him. Like me. I thought about trying to get the attention of one of the MARTA police, but realized that by the time I explained what was going on, it might be too late.

I made it to the top of the escalator before I caught sight of Dykstra again. He was already close to the bottom, worming his way around the people standing still on the steps. As I followed down, I could now see over the heads of travelers who hemmed me in. The crowd on the platform thinned out as people moved away from the escalator. Paul had already made it close to the far end of the platform, where he was leaning a little forward, peering into the tunnel. He must have heard, as I did, the first gentle roar of an approaching train. Then I spotted Tanello. He was about half way between Paul and Dykstra, who was now moving swiftly along the platform in pursuit. I had no doubt it was Tanello, even though I could only see his back. Average height, ordinary brown hair, an unexceptional camel hair jacket, but the way he moved – like a cat – gave him away, that and the way the jacket was cut to downplay muscular shoulders and neck. Or was there a sense of evil that emanated from him like an aura? In any event, I recognized him, and for a sickening second I was convinced he knew I was there too, and that he was smiling.

I reached the bottom of the escalator and again my lack of stature prevented me from seeing what was happening down the platform. I dodged and weaved through the people, conscious of a crescendo of noise from the approaching train. Then a single scream cut through the racket, rapidly followed by the jarring metal screech of brakes. A woman staggered past me, her face ashen, eyes wide.

"A man under the train! He just–" She gulped, then stumbled on, perhaps searching for a police officer, or for a place to be sick. I started running forward again. Then there was no one between me and the tableau at the end of the platform: Paul spread-eagled on the ground, and Dykstra bent over him. I arrived, breathless, as Dykstra pulled Paul to his feet.

"Are you both alright? Where is he?"

I turned to follow their gaze back behind me. There was an eerie stillness to the scene. The train had come to a stop about a third of the way along the platform. The driver must have been in shock still sitting in the cab. The train doors remained closed. People stood back, mouths open, trying to grasp what had happened. In a few moments, activity would resume. The MARTA police would arrive, the train would have to be moved, its captive passengers released, the platform cleared. Then, the grizzly task of removing the remains. Witnesses would be interviewed, including Paul, Dykstra and myself. IDs checked; explanations offered. But for now, the three of us stood supporting each other, taking deep shuddering breaths.

Paul was the first to speak.

"You saved my life, man," He giggled hysterically. "I mean, you really did!"

Dykstra shrugged, and I couldn't help thinking of Harrison Ford in those old Indiana Jones films as he spoke.

"Paul, looks like you're going to miss your plane after all."

Give him a fedora and a whip, shout "Action!" and he was your ready-made hero, complete with self-deprecatory throw-away lines. I was torn between stamping my foot in frustration at his foolhardiness, and swooning into his arms like a silent movie actress. Damn the man, I loved him.

**

It was after midnight when we got back to Decatur. We were both drained of any desire to talk, having been interviewed to the point of exhaustion over the last five hours so my planned tête à tête did not take place.

Initially, two uniformed MARTA police had escorted us to their precinct discreetly located on the street level of the station. Paul was led off to a separate office, but I stridently insisted that I was Dykstra's lawyer and he had the right to my presence regardless of whether he was going to be charged with anything. They gave way reluctantly, without commenting on the serendipitous coincidence that the perpetrator had his attorney standing by when he pushed someone under a train. It turned out that their questioning was preliminary anyway: name, address, who, what, where, when, how. Dykstra told them who Tanello was, and why he had targeted Paul, but these guys seemed unimpressed. It turned out that they were waiting for an Atlanta PD homicide detective, who arrived about the time Paul's plane was supposed to take off for Paris.

The APD detective took Dykstra through the whole story again, probing for details in a way I could see Dykstra approved. I said little. I had not witnessed Tanello go under the train, but I did confirm that I thought it was him heading down the platform towards Paul, and about Paul's role as a grand jury witness against him. Once the federal involvement was laid out, the detective withdrew to "make some calls" and probably cross-check our information with Paul's story.

Soon after that, some familiar faces from the FBI turned up. Our savior, Agent Mel Harbrough, now dressed in a conservative dark suit, blue shirt and tie, was his usually restrained self, acknowledging us with a nod but keeping his lips pursed in a thin line. The agent I assumed to be his boss was a little more forthcoming. He had evidently been the one to question Dykstra in Jacksonville. They shook hands, if not like old friends, then without hostility, and he turned to me.

"Ms. McKinney, I'm Jackson Blewitt, the agent in charge of the investigation. You two have had quite an exciting few days, I understand. The MARTA folks and the Atlanta PD have agreed to release Mr. Dykstra here into the FBI's custody. They're not charging him with anything, at least at present, based on several witnesses' statements that he pushed Mr. Tanello aside only to prevent him from attacking Paul Yusef who, as you know, is a material witness against Mr. Tanello in my ongoing investigation. Well, probably not ongoing in light of Mr. Tanello's death." Blewitt sighed. It had probably been a long day for him too. "It isn't the way I wanted to wind up this case. Too many loose ends. In fact, it's a mess."

"But why is Pieter being handed over to you, if he's not being charged with anything." I was getting steamed up again, memories of that Florida beach at dawn, Dykstra being bundled into a sedan and whisked away. However, the subject of my protest seemed to accept his fate happily, standing up and stretching to get the kinks out of his shoulders.

"Loose ends. Ms. McKinney. I need Mr. Dykstra's statement, and Mr. Yusef's too. We can take care of it tonight if y'all will come back with me and Agent Harbrough to the Federal Building. Otherwise, it'll just take up time tomorrow, and I understand that the young man is eager to catch a flight back to the Middle East, so best to get it done tonight."

So the three of us, plus Agents Harbrough and Blewitt piled into a town car for the short drive back to the FBI's offices in the Federal Building. There, Paul was again led off to a separate office to give his statement to Agent Harbrough, while Dykstra and I were questioned by Agent Blewitt. As he had the benefit of both the MARTA cops' and the APD detective's notes, this was efficiently done. Blewitt left to arrange for the statements to be typed up. When we had read, revised and signed them, there was just time enough to catch the last train from Five Points to Decatur.

Chapter 20

Dykstra spread butter methodically on the toasted bagel, took a bite, then laid it back deliberately in the center of the plate, all without raising his eyes to me. I stood watching him, standing with my back to the sink, my arms folded across my stomach, hiding my nervously clenching fists. I knew he was as conscious of the minutes clicking by on the kitchen clock as I was, even though he kept his gaze stubbornly in front of him.

When I purchased the clock – a piece of 1950's whimsy with an oval red and white gingham frame and stylized spoons for hands - I thought it was amusingly kitsch, and would lighten the mood in my otherwise streamlined kitchen. Now its jolly tick-tock jarred with the melancholy that draped over the room like a shroud, mocking me for my doomed attempt at playfulness.

"There's no need to drive me to the airport. I'll take MARTA." He spoke softly, still without looking at me.

"No, let me drive you. It's no bother; the worst of the morning traffic will be over." I wanted to keep him with me as long as possible, but there was also a part of me that wanted to make sure he actually boarded that plane. Even now, I was unsure of him. It was not a question of trust, after everything we had gone through together, Lelana's death, our kidnapping and torture, the final mad underground chase. It was just that he was unpredictable, subject to rapid changes of direction that left me, a left-brained linear thinker, spinning in his wake. Now that it was decided that he was leaving, I needed to turn the page, get back to my life, however boring I anticipated that life would seem.

"OK, but ...." He did look up then, and the hurt in his eyes made me turn away. I stared out of the window at the back yard, swallowing tears. It was an overcast day, and a mean little wind was worrying the leaves that had fallen from the oak tree. I should have raked them up weeks ago, I thought. Well, I'd have time for that now.

Dykstra continued to munch his bagel, and I fussed with the coffee pot and wiped up non-existent marks from the countertop. We didn't speak. I wondered if this was how old married couples ate their breakfast: bound together by time and habit, but each immersed in their own silence. I guessed I would never know.

We had nothing left to say to each other. Yesterday, we had said it all, talked it out from every angle, angry at one moment, tender the next. We talked about our feelings for each other, careful to avoid the L word. We compared our careers, competing subtly, then not so subtly, over the demanding nature of our jobs and the sacrifices we had made on the path to professional success. We analyzed our contrasting personality types, deciding he was a Meyers Briggs extravert: intuitive and feeling, while I was an introvert, judging and sensing. We argued over politics: my "liberal" opinions sounding right-of-center to him, but both of us glad to find unity on issues like gay rights and global warming. Then we circled back to our relationship: the difficulty of it, living on two continents, working as hard as we did. A long distance friendship wasn't enough; a commitment was too much.

After dinner, I opened another bottle of the Central Coast cabernet sauvignon we had drunk with the pork tenderloin and roasted vegetables.

"If only we had met twenty years ago, before we got so .... independent!" He said, smiling ruefully. We were sitting close together on the sofa. He was twisting a lock of my hair round his finger. I rested my head back against his hand, closed my eyes, and contemplated my younger self.

"God, no! I was a wounded animal, snarling at anyone who tried to come close."

"Wounded? How?" His voice was a seductive whisper. I teetered on the brink of telling him what I had resisted disclosing to any human soul, even my therapist: the squalor and neglect, the violent rows fueled by alcohol and whatever drugs my parents could lay their hands on. And the darker secret, buried now so deep that I wondered if it really happened, or was it just an echo of a childhood nightmare, or the half-remembered rumor about another girl, not me at all? I stood on that figurative cliff and peered into the void of "after": after I revealed my past. I saw Dykstra recoil, the concern in his eyes turn to pity, and then to disgust. I sat forward abruptly and picked up my glass.

"Unhappy childhood." I answered shortly, and took a long swallow of wine.

Sometime after midnight, we collapsed into bed, clinging to each other like the exhausted survivors of a terrible shipwreck, washed up on some deserted island. We lay there for ages, too tired even to sleep. Eventually, I felt the soft sweep of his thumb down my neck from under my ear to my collarbone, again and again. Like an obedient animal, my body slowly relaxed and conformed more pliantly to his. Our lovemaking was a requiem, a remembrance of what might have been; sadness and passion, human connection across a universe of empty space.

"Sarah, I want you to know that I—" I put my hand over his mouth. I didn't need to hear a declaration of love. The wetness on his cheeks was enough.

***

I spent the day preparing for an upcoming mediation. It was my favorite kind of case. Basically, a property dispute

199

between two branches of the same family, but it led me into realms of law of which I had no prior knowledge: nineteenth century tribal treaties, up-state mining rights - who knew there was bauxite under Buffalo? And yet the case revealed some universal human quandaries: a daughter damaged by the knowledge that her father wanted a son; a would-be artist yearning to be free of the corporate straightjacket imposed by his family's wealth.

It was after dark when I emerged from my office into the living room. Face to face with the computer screen, I had missed the few hours of weak February sunshine that may have signaled the change from winter into spring. I turned on lights and heated water for tea, then settled onto the sofa and reached for the remote.

For years I had rejected the idea of owning a television. I got my news from National Public Radio, or, more recently, from newspaper internet feeds. I went to the movies I wanted to see, and felt no need to get addicted to series or sitcoms that pictured a lifestyle with which I had nothing in common. But I had bought this handsome flat-screen, wall-mounted model as a present to myself for Christmas, telling myself I needed to get more in touch with popular culture. How could I relate to my clients if I didn't understand their American Idol references, or know what celebrity was baring their soul to Oprah?

If I was honest, the real reason for buying the TV was a need to be a spectator, no matter how remotely, of Dykstra's world. I had not heard from him – or him from me – since the day seventeen weeks ago (but who was counting?) that I had said goodbye to him at Hartsfield-Jackson Atlanta Airport, but my few hectic weeks with him had given me a taste for international political intrigue; since Christmas, I had become a CNN junkie. Now, armed with lemon ginger tea and a handful of Belgian almond cookies, I prepared to scan the globe.

Anderson Cooper was reporting from Egypt. He was silhouetted against the night sky – it must be after midnight there –

with the outline of the Pyramids behind him. What had started as a minor protest in Tunisia was now spreading, as people took to the streets all over the Middle East. Several thousand were occupying Tahrir Square in Cairo. After first dismissing the protesters as criminals and drug addicts, President Mubarak had promised reforms, if only the people would be patient. Now nothing would satisfy the mob except his ouster. And not just Mubarak, but his spokesmen, allies and family members – some of whose names I had become acquainted with in the course of our investigation. Well, Dykstra's investigation.

"When we come back, I'll be talking to a journalist who has spent the last year tracking Mubarak's millions – money laundering on a grand scale – and there's an American connection!"

I nearly spilt my tea. He had to be talking about Dykstra! In one of those inset boxes on the bottom right that CNN is so fond of, I saw a familiar face before the screen went to black. I sat tensely through the commercials, afraid to take my eyes away from inane ads for products no one needed in case I missed anything. Then Anderson Cooper was back, this time the background was the ancient Sphinx. Cooper's intense blue eyes looked directly into mine.

"Pieter Dykstra is a Dutch investigative journalist who has tracked how Middle-Eastern strongmen such as Mubarak have smuggled their wealth into other countries."

The shot widened to include the man next to Cooper. I couldn't suppress a gasp. It was unreal: there was Dykstra, more tanned, his grey hair grown out of the buzz cut he had worn the previous fall and curling attractively over his ears. He was silhouetted against the backdrop of an indigo sky and the floodlit ruin of a three thousand year old monument. My throat closed and breathing became an effort as I waited to hear his voice. Stupid, stupid me. I could be with him there in Egypt, watching history being made. Or at least, I could be a cell phone call away in the London flat with its spectacular view, part of his life, with advance notice of his CNN appearance.

"So, Pieter, how did Mubarak and his circle manage to hide their assets?"

That smile. I held my mug in a death grip, afraid to move a muscle.

"Well, after September 11 it became harder to hide money in foreign bank accounts, such as Swiss numbered accounts, so these rulers had to find other ways to protect their wealth. They started investing in "black diamonds" – illegally mined gems from West Africa - and using a network of smugglers to take them to Europe and eventually Antwerp to sell them on the diamond market there. Associates would then invest the proceeds in legitimate companies. The problem was that organized crime groups got wind of the trade, and demanded a cut."

"You mean the Mafia?"

"Yes, that was one group. There were others. They demanded a commission for "protecting" the smuggled shipments as they traveled through southern Europe."

"And what about this American connection?"

"The plan was to avoid having to pay off the European crime families. Plus there was the danger of swamping the Antwerp market. A new smuggling route was developed to New York where there is an equally vital diamond exchange. When a shipment went astray, the criminals at the US end – criminals who were being tracked by the FBI – turned violent. Lives were lost."

"I understand you were in some personal danger yourself."

"Yes." Dykstra turned towards the camera at this point. *"If it was not for the bravery of a beautiful woman I would not be alive today."* Me? He was talking about me? I burst out laughing.

Then, as I realized the implications, my jaw dropped. Cooper was still smiling.

"Well, that sounds like a great adventure. You have a book coming out, I believe?"

"Yes. "The Riddle of the Sphinx" comes out in the US in May. It tells the whole story." Again, Dykstra turned his gaze away from Anderson Cooper and spoke directly to me. I barely heard the wrap-up and handover back to the CNN studio in Atlanta.

"You bastard!" I yelled futilely at the TV. "You dirty rotten-- urgh!" How could he expose me like that? He knew it would ruin my professional reputation as a serious mediator if I was named in some true-life adventure story with diamond smuggling and organized crime syndicates. I threw the remote across the room. If he was here this minute, I would strangle him! What was he thinking? I'd have to go to the publishers in New York, stop the publication somehow.

Or I could go to London and confront him there. Tell him he had to edit out any reference to me, or ..... what? I'd sue? And achieve the same notoriety as he was threatening with his tell-all book?

Suddenly, I saw it all clearly. I smiled and stretched out on the sofa like a cat. He wanted to send me a message. Too proud himself to violate our agreement that we would make a clean break, he was using an international cable news network to provoke me into doing it. He knew I would be so incensed by the idea of exposure that I wouldn't be able to resist reaching out.

The bastard .....

FOR MORE ABOUT THE AUTHOR AND THE SARAH
MCKINNEY SERIES

Check in with www.marianexall.com